U

the

Olive Tree

Bédar Writers

Under the Olive Tree

Acknowledgements

Each of the contributions in this anthology was shared with the Bédar Writers group, redrafted and then submitted to select friends and family to be proofread. Our thanks go to all those who helped fashion the final submissions.

We are especially grateful to the Gonzalez Garcia family from the Bar El Cortijo in Bédar who allow us to use their dining room each week.

Estamos especialmente agradecidos con la familia González García del bar Cortijo dc Bédar que permiten utilizar sus comedor cada semana.

Contents

v

Under the Olive Tree

Glenis Meeks

Under the olive tree
writers' minds meet.
Words discussed.
Formats hammered,
beaten and shaped,
emerging polished,
honed. Fresh.

Stories diverse pour
from printed pages.
Articles, anecdotes
nature observed.
Irony, mystery,
farcical comedy.
Collected, assessed,
tempered, compiled.

What is the purpose?
What is the goal
of this torrent of talent
so resolutely cast?
Pleasure for writer.
Delight for reader.
A fusion formed
under the olive tree.

A Bédar Goat Tale

Tony Carter

'Hola, Pedro.'
'Hola, amigo.'
'¿Todos bien?'
'Sí, bien ¿y para ti?
It was the usual familiar greeting.

Pedro was a young guy, tall and lean. He had been educated and could have moved to a well-paid job in Almería but he preferred the family business and village life. He was accompanied by about forty goats of various sizes and colours and half a dozen odd-looking sheep.

A scruffy dog responded to a sharp 'Fran!' and all manner of whistles, clicks and other utterances that came from Pedro. But, of course, the goats and sheep understood perfectly.

They moved individually in a stuttered, jerky manner but as a group they seemed to flow, now to one side of the *barranco* where there was a large patch of chard, the wild spinach-like plant that grows so well in the Bédar area.

The goats tucked into the chard - a real treat. By now the sun beat down and the swifts and swallows started scooping the flying insects from the warm sky. Aromas blended and drifted past, mixtures of herbs and flowers. Blossom and even the goats contributed to the potpourri of exotic fragrances. The sun beamed through the orange and lemon trees, with sparkling reflections from the shiny leaves.

Having finished their meal, the goats continued downhill, their bells clinking as they went. Pedro called out to Ramón, walking his donkey to the *fuente* for some free mountain water.

The bell of the church clock clanged loudly; it was ten o'clock. Then there was a period of quiet. By now many people had dispersed to bars *El Paso*, *El Cortijo*, or *El Empalme*, to consume that vital morning coffee or brandy.

This was not the Spain of the *costas*, but the real rural heart of a thriving village. The only sounds now those created by nature.

Miguel, a late middle-aged, grossly overweight villager and his dog, Chico, edged down the *barranco* for the morning gathering of chard leaves. He suddenly stopped and looked stunned, unable to believe his eyes. Instantly, he realized that the lush green leaves had been replaced by a generous scattering of telltale brown ball bullets that goats leave everywhere they go.

He swore aloud and then he heard that unmistakeable clunk of a distant goat bell.

'Come on, Chico. We are going to have some words with Pedro.'

After five minutes of stumbling over rocks, they caught up with the goats, which were by now milling around the van beside the goat shed. Pedro was loading up cheeses for delivery along the eastern coast of Andalucía.

'Hey, Pedro, your goats have eaten all the chard.'

'Yeah, they were hungry.'

'So am I,' replied Miguel. 'My hens are laying well and I have a nice bit of *jamón* to put with the chard in a tortilla. I was really looking forward to it.'

'Well you'll just have to wait for it to grow,' laughed Pedro.

His laughter was misjudged and it inflamed Miguel. It was as if he were taunting him. The argument quickly escalated.

'Selfish bastard. Your family always were selfish back-stabbers.'

Initially, Pedro felt hurt at these comments and responded angrily.

'Your family were always stabbed in the back because they were always running away.'

These inferences always drifted back to past conflicts. There had been dreadful times for everyone. If you wanted to insult someone you referred to that period and their family involvement. Most people had something to hide, something they were ashamed of.

By now Miguel was at boiling point. He ran at Pedro, who was ready for him. He quickly sidestepped and Miguel fell flat on the ground. He was slow to rise.

'Time to calm things down, my friend,' said Pedro. Despite his slight build, he was young and very fit.

Miguel was not yet ready for conciliation. '*Hijo de puta*.' You son of a prostitute.

'Look,' said Pedro, 'that chard is not on anybody's land. It's there for anyone. It's just as

10

much mine as yours. Anyway, there must be some more elsewhere.'

Miguel was not appeased. 'You led your goats here so they would eat it and deprive me.'

'Don't be so ridiculous, Miguel. You know that we wander all around the village, different areas on different days.'

By now Miguel was fully upright. He was a big man but overweight and unfit. The stuffing had been knocked out of him but he was still angry. However, in truth, he didn't know what to say or do. He just stood glowering at the younger man.

Pedro seized the initiative. 'Look, come on. Let's forget this now. Come to the goat shed later and I'll give you some cheese – the tortilla will be just as good with some nice fresh goat's cheese, if not better.'

Miguel remained silent, trying to work out a response without loss of face. This simple dispute could go on literally for years; a friend here would normally be for life, but so could an enemy. It could even pass to the next generation. He knew also in his heart that Pedro was right and being reasonable, but it was hard to swallow.

Reluctantly he grunted assent as he brushed his clothes down.

Later Miguel tried the cheese and grudgingly admitted that it was good.

Pedro just couldn't resist. 'You may find it has a slight flavour of chard,' he said.

Market Day

Jean McGrane

Maggie flopped down onto the seat next to her daughter with a loud sigh. It was a relief to be out of the rain even if it had made her breathless rushing to catch the bus. She was glad that she had decided to leave early: the weather had spoiled the market and the stallholders looked as if they were preparing to pack up. Now she was ready to be home, out of her wet things and with a cup of tea in front of the fire.

She took off her plastic rainy day bonnet and snapped the two taped ends together sending droplets onto the floor. Mrs Thwaites was rocking her large bulk up the aisle, her bulging bags making her passage through the bus even more difficult. To make extra room, Maggie squeezed up to her daughter who shifted in her seat but seemed intent on playing with the raindrops on the steamed up window.

There was the usual good humour and joking with the bus conductor as he collected their fares.

'Come on, let's get this crate moving before we all catch pneumonia.'

'What a wash out.'

'Aye, I'm soaked right through.'

As the bus pulled away, Maggie settled her bag more firmly on her knee and assessed the contents.

'Bread, a piece of brisket for Sunday, Janet's shoes…Maybe I'll get the plants next week. Not bad, considering.'

Her expression changed as she remembered that morning's argument. It was always the same on Tuesdays. She dreaded it coming. Living in a small village and with no car there weren't many opportunities to get out to the shops. Market day could have been a bright spot in the week but there was always the battle over money.

'Reg, can I have some money for Hawes?'

'I haven't got much. I'll need some for the auction mart.'

'Well give me £5. I need shoes for Janet from Brian's stall today and I want some plants if they have some.'

Then came the stubbornness, the frustration, the angry words and finally the ungracious settlement at £3. Remembering how she had snatched the money from his hand and stormed out of the house, Maggie carried on the argument in her own head, '£3 to cover bus fares, fish and chips and his brown bread leaving nothing else for the rest of the shopping. And I have Janet with me this week. It's lucky I make a few bob from the school canteen - a job he didn't want me to take.'

Maggie casually, in mid thought, leaned over to Janet who was drawing stick men on the steamy window and knocked her hand down.

'Don't make a mess. It'll leave greasy marks when it dries.'

She felt Janet's skinny frame tense next to her and reached out to squeeze her hand. It was icy cold. 'Here, give me your hands to rub,' she said, 'Now look at them raindrops. I'm choosing that big fat one. Which one do you want? Let's have a race to see which one gets to the bottom first.'

The driver closed the bus door and began to cautiously steer through the pedestrians, unheeding now in their dash to get out of the sudden downpour.

'Mam, I think that's Daddy.'

Maggie looked to where Janet was pointing and saw Reg running towards the bus, his flat cap pulled low over his face and his coat collar turned up in futile defence against the deluge. He had his hand out to stop the bus but the driver, trying to clear the steam from his windscreen hadn't spotted him.

Maggie tensed her body to shout for the bus to stop but then sat back in her seat.

'I don't think he's ready to come home yet. He'll still have to go to the auction mart.'

She reached into the top of her bag and took a slightly damp comic out of the top. She passed it across and was rewarded with a quiet smile.

'Such a reader that girl,' she thought. At least there had been a few coppers for that.

She looked across the aisle to where Mrs Thwaites was shaking the rain off her headscarf.

'What a day,' she said. 'You could nearly catch your death of cold.'

El Camino de Los Peregrinos

MarianMay Simpson

Eileen's feet shot from beneath her as she slipped on the loose stones and landed in a tangled heap at the bottom of the slope. 'It could not get much worse,' she thought to herself, as she struggled to pull herself off her weighted rucksack. Only the first day and our pilgrims were already hours behind schedule having walked in a complete circle in the wrong direction.

This was July 2013 and local women from Bédar, friends Eileen Kilmurry and Sheila Turner, were just beginning the first stage of their one hundred and thirty kilometre journey along *The Way of St James* or the *Camino de Santiago de Compostela.*

'Keep the sun behind you,' they had been told and 'you will always be going west.' They had missed the yellow arrows, which mark *The Way* and had been sent in the wrong direction by two workmen. The cry of '*Buen Camino*' from the passers by was clearly not working for them. Eileen did not see the funny side at first as Sheila had to unhook her from her rucksack so she could haul herself off the ground and nurse her bruised knees.

Sheila was sufficiently sympathetic considering she had her own problems. Her feet were already hot and blistering after only one day's walking. It was important, according to the guidebooks, to wear socks made of natural fibres and to change them every hour, drying them tied to their rucksack as they walked along.

They managed to reach the *Refugio* or *Alberque,* with no hope of a bed due to the lateness of their arrival, and took the thin rubber gym mat offered and joined the other thirty five unfortunates on the floor of the local church. The poor man's meal of rice and tomatoes was followed by a brief night's sleep, accompanied by the constant chime of the church bells overhead and someone singing below the window. They had to ask themselves if they had signed up for this when Eileen had a membership card for the *Parador* Hotel Group somewhere at home.

They knew that these *hostals*, or places of refuge, were not renowned for their luxury accommodation, but offered just one night of rest for a minimum fee or donation to all travellers carrying the Pilgrims passport or *Credencial.* On arrival, the pilgrims had to queue for an available bed or continue on to the next *Refugio*, which could be a further five or ten kilometres walk. They were not given sheets, only a mattress and a pillow, so they had to carry their own sleeping bags where they hid any valuables at night. The number of bunks to a room varied from three to forty-five depending on the standard of the *hostal*. Often a kitchen was available for cooking, but our intrepid travellers settled for wine, salad and tapas in the nearby bar. They were allowed one shower each, although often the hot water had long since run out, so they had to be content with cold. Hair washing was difficult, especially without a hairdryer and curling tongs.

Undeterred, they continued on their journey at half past three the next morning, after a meagre breakfast of bread and biscuits, stopping at the nearest *farmacia* for knee bandages, blister pads and a few painkilling remedies.

Logroño, along the *Camino Francés,* was their starting point and, as the capital of *La Rioja* wine region, promised to provide some welcome treats at the end of the day, and at half the price charged in the local bars back home in Bédar. Sadly, not enough room in the rucksack for a couple of bottles to help ease the pain.

They realised quite quickly how important it was not to carry too much weight in the rucksack, as it caused more, nasty blisters. They each carried only two sets of clothing, which they were able to wash each day at the *Alberque*. One set was kept for walking, which they slept in at night, ready to leave quietly each morning while it was still dark, picking up their boots, left at the door overnight to dry out.

The Way of St James was one of the most important Christian pilgrimages during medieval times, beginning at *St Jean Pied de Port* in France and ending at the Pilgrimage site of *Santiago de Compostela,* North Western Spain (a total of around eight hundred kilometres), where the body of the Apostle James was allegedly buried. The Christian martyr had been beheaded in Palestine on the orders of King Herod and his body was miraculously carried on a boat steered by angels, to the Galician coast, where a church was built at the place where the body was found.

The pilgrimage was sometimes made as a penance, or for enlightenment, and began traditionally from one's home. To this day, travellers of all faiths, from all over the world, undertake *The Way* for spiritual or religious reasons, joining and leaving the path at different points, and stopping to have the *Credencial* stamped as proof of their arduous journey. The yellow arrows and the scallop shell motif point the direction, and water is left outside the houses for the passing pilgrims. The symbol of the *Camino de Santiago*, the scallop shell, marks *The Way* and, traditionally, those who returned from *Compostela* would carry a shell back home as proof of their journey. According to one legend, the body of Saint James was found covered in scallop shells and this has since become an important motif to celebrate the journey in his honour.

If travellers want to focus totally on the journey, they are advised to leave behind their watches, mobile phones and cameras. Some pilgrims, mainly students, took the bus, only walking a short distance, claiming the stamp to their passport falsely, arriving first at the *Alberque* and always sure of a bed for the night. Our *Peregrinos* took their pilgrimage seriously and wanted to do this for the experience, whilst also raising money for charity. They had a lot of fun, and laughs, yet found it a very humbling experience.

They met some interesting people. From Seoul, Korea; a 71 year old widower from Chicago; two children and a loud gregarious woman who walked very little and practiced Thai Chi every morning; an Englishman, who took his dog with him, but was unable to take it in the *Alberque* and was forced to spend his nights outside. He told them many stories relating to the sad life he had led. Sheila noticed that he had brought more equipment with him for his dog than for himself.

After the third day's walk, Eileen was suffering from her knee injuries and Sheila had finally to admit defeat and visit the Medical Centre because the soles of her feet were covered in blisters and in danger of becoming infected. She subsequently lost two of her toenails. Many travellers do not finish their journey due to their injuries and are sent home by the Doctors.

Sheila's feet were so bad, she was not allowed to walk for the rest of the trip and Eileen had to continue the rest of the arduous journey alone. It was lonely without her friend and she had many tough days with a lot of climbing. She met up with Sheila on the seventh day at the bus station in Burgos, where they had a last blissful night in a Hotel. Eileen enjoyed a long awaited trip to the hairdressers before they headed home for Bédar.

Eileen and Sheila are both farmers' daughters who get on well and share the same sense of discipline and commitment to anything they decide to do. They are both keen walkers who get up each morning and walk at least ten kilometres in the mountains near home.

19

In spite of the harshness of the pilgrimage they have decided to finish the whole of the *Camino* over the next two years, completing it in 2015. They will both arrive at the pilgrimage site at *Santiago de Campostela* as very fit seventy year olds!

The Cat

Michael Palmer

'Thomas! Come on, it's starting to snow again. Let's get home as quickly as we can,' urged his mum.

Thomas, being an emotionally intelligent six-year old, could read his mum well. As an act of defiance, but not over doing it, he kicked at the lower branches of a snow-covered bush causing a cascade of white flakes to fall onto his boots. A movement in the bush caught his eye and very gingerly, putting one paw in front of the other, a small cat moved from the cover of the bush.

'Stop!' shouted Thomas startling Em, his mum, and frightening the kitten, which as a protective gesture moved deeper back into the bush.

'We are going to get frozen if you don't hurry up.' And, retracing her steps, Em took a firm hold on Thomas' hand and marched the pair of them determinately towards home, through the increasingly deepening snow.

'Stop!' shouted Thomas again.

His exasperated mother turned and said, 'What on earth is the matter?'

'Look a small cat,' said Thomas. 'It's lost, cold and lonely.'

'No it's not. It probably lives in one of these houses and will soon want to make its way back to it's nice warm home.'

Unconvinced, but not wanting to challenge his mother any further, he walked - or rather was pulled by her as she tried to increase the pace homewards. Every chance he got, he looked back and that acted as a brake on the urgent pace his mum was trying to set.

A small black blob was clearly visible in the snow, sometimes above the snow and sometimes below it, but clearly following Thomas and his mum. The battle of wills set in as Thomas stated the obvious and his mother ignored the remarks knowing, with a sinking feeling, where they were headed.

'It's following us,' said Thomas. 'We should help it.'

'Yes, we should,' said his mum, 'but it knows where it is and will soon turn round and go home.' It was one of those statements with more hope than fact, and the fact was that the kitten was following them with little intention of turning round, however much his mother willed it.

Encouraged by the determination of the kitten and the resignation he detected in his mum's voice, Thomas talked up the need to love animals and help them whenever possible. A friendly Vicar, who had taken the school assembly few days ago, had made this exact point and had seemed to gain the approval of all whom Thomas regarded as figures of authority, including his teacher. It seemed an appropriate time to remind his mother of this message, which was not well received by her.

'We do love animals,' she said, 'but it's best the kitten goes back to those who love him. Just think how much they must be missing it.'

Thomas felt a strange conflict. He loved his mum and was able to communicate with her in many ways. Laughter, play, sharing with her his interest in dinosaurs, and the total commitment he gave in building complex Lego models. They were all channels that bonded them into their secure and close relationship. Thomas instinctively knew he was right and his mum was wrong, even though she seemed so certain.

Why was his mum so against the cat?

The snow was blowing directly into their faces and the cold of the snow and wind, which seemed to rise out of nowhere, made them cuddle together and press on towards home. As they turned into their road - lined with houses and parked cars - even Thomas was glad to be back and the lights in their house seemed to welcome them home. In the shelter of the front door, mother and son quickly took off their boots and coats and tumbled inside, but not before Thomas heard a low meow.

'It's Cat,' said Thomas and, not waiting for any approval from his mum, he scooped up the cat and put him on the hall floor.

Three pairs of eyes looked down on a small piece of fur (with a dash of white on top) shivering with cold and dehydration. Thomas closed the door and looked at the two most important people in his life: Em, his mum, and Frances, his grandmother.

He pleaded the case for Cat to stay at least for the night. The case for the prosecution was clear,

23

starting from 'Why did you bring it home?' to 'Its owner will be out looking for it...' to 'What are we going to give it to eat and drink?'

But Thomas ignored these questions and, with a simple statement, he trumped their tricks.

'Well you can't throw it out!'

And against such simple logic, the opposition collapsed and the two ladies started the practical steps required to secure the little animals needs and comfort. Firstly, a towel to dry the cat (much against its wishes). Secondly, some milk, which brought approval in the form of purring And finally, mince, which was eagerly consumed and the cat then curled up by the stove and fell asleep.

The next morning brought one of those glorious sunny winter days. No wind, but the countryside was covered with a blanket of snow that was piling up against doors and windows and covering cars. The traditional British approach to such a sudden touch of winter was observed: a long list of school closures over the radio; roads fit for travel 'only if your journey is really necessary'; shops stripped of all food in preparation for a siege that would certainly last all of two days.

Thomas enjoyed the bonus day, off school with his new friend. He wasn't sure how to approach the subject of the new arrival and decided on a soft, persuasive touch.

'What a lovely cat' and 'Don't you like cats?' seemed good openers.

Cat was thoroughly domesticated and would scratch at the door to be let out. There was no problem fitting into the neighbourhood as the garden and adjoining fields would become its natural territory.

Realising they were faced with a fait accompli, Mother and Grandmother took a realistic look at the options. Clearly the cat belonged to another family who might be missing it. They needed to publicise that they had the cat and see what the response was and, in turn, return it to its rightful owner.

There are people in any village who are the communicators. They know where to go for the best builders, plumbers, electricians, the best shops and associated bargains. If you need to know something, this is where you went and, even on a personal level, what they seemed to know about village life could be very revealing. And so Frances called her friend Ruby, an unimpeachable source of such information, to say that she would like to call in for a chat.

'It would be lovely to see you tomorrow, my dear,' said Ruby. 'Do you want to come for lunch?'

'I would love to but I think I only have time for a cup of tea and a chat.'

The next day, the two friends met up and, over a steaming cup of tea, it only took a few minutes to update Ruby. 'Sounds like a lovely cat and just the kind of cat anyone would like to have as a pet,' said Ruby

'The last thing we need is a cat. The guinea pig keeps us fully occupied on the animal front. If we take on another pet, just think of the costs. Vet's bills cost a fortune, and its food, and all the other bits and pieces would put more pressure on an already tight budget. Finding the owner would suit us all round all – well, except for Thomas who has fallen in love with the cat.'

'I haven't heard of anyone who has lost a kitten but I'll keep my ears open. Let me bring you up to date with goings on. But, before that, another cup of tea or something a stronger. A glass of sherry my son gave me? I happen to know it's very good.'

'Ruby, I have to go to the post office to put this card advertising the lost cat, and then a couple of posters on telegraph poles in the village. I don't want to be arrested for being drunk and disorderly.'

'At our age its one of the few pleasures left, so let's drink and be damned.'

'Just the one, then,' said Frances, knowing that, if she wasn't careful, half the bottle would be downed in an instant...But it was in a good cause, wasn't it?

An hour later – and feeling distinctly warmer and lightheaded – she set off for the post office.

'Do you want the card in for a week or a fortnight?' said the Postmistress. 'I haven't heard that anyone has lost a cat, but best make it a fortnight...' She then added a statement that implied anything less would be a waste of time and therefore money.

'A fortnight it is,' said Frances, 'and please would you give me a call if you hear anyone who has lost a cat?'

'OK,' said the postmistress.

Frances set off quickly, to make up for lost time. 'It's funny how can you lose time and yet you can make up for it,' she philosophised on the way home, mulling over the events that brought Cat into their lives. 'We don't need a cat, but I have to admit this one has fitted into our lives, won our hearts and become a family member...'

Later that afternoon, she picked up Thomas from school and the two of them walked home silently. Both, it seems, were thinking about the same subject...

Thomas was anxious to get home as quickly as possible to greet his new friend and Frances, being more practical, wondered how things were going to work out.

Thomas opened the front door and called out, 'Where are you Cat?'

Both were happy to see each other and, after the initial bonding, Thomas gave his new friend a saucer of milk (this, with the admonition of his grandmother who had just given Cat a saucer of milk!)

No matter, this was Thomas' milk, with that added ingredient of care.

After such care, Cat slipped out the back door, leaving the comfort of home to go hunting in the adjacent fields - a pastime that lasted well into the night and often into the next day.

When the two weeks were up and there had been no response to the advertisement, it was removed from the shop window and Cat was officially declared the fourth member of the household, much to Thomas' relief and delight.

*

'No Cat?' said Thomas next morning, as rushing to get ready for school as departure time got closer. Cries of…'Have you got your lunch?' and 'You've left your homework on the table!' and 'Why don't you want to go to Karate club after school?' Then, with the flash of brake lights, a hoot on the horn, and a squeal of tyres, they finally got away.

Frances sat down at the computer to start a day's work, which continued until broken by the lunchtime arrival of her daughter.

'Has Cat reappeared?' said Em.

'Not yet,' replied Frances.

'Seems to have been away for a longer time than usual.'

'Yes, but cats are a bit like that,' said Frances

'Oh well, maybe it's found its way home. Any news from your publicity of a lost cat?'

'Not a whisper.'

'Well, it looks like it's going to be a permanent fixture here then. Better start to think about a name,' said Em.

'I supposed so,' replied Frances, in a resigned reply. 'I'm off, back to work. You OK to pick Thomas up?'

'Yes should be OK. The weather's clearing. I might take the bike so Thomas can ride home.'

'Thanks Mum. Off now. See you later.'

Frances made her way along the pleasant tree lined lane surrounded, on both sides, by fields that led to the school. This was a quiet part of the English countryside, allowing just a few minutes peace before the next energy discharge released by the fifty excited children waiting for their parents.

'My bike!' cried Thomas. 'To ride home on. You are the best granny in the whole world.' This was confirmed by the sudden, speedy departure of Thomas on his bike, homeward bound.

'Slow down Thomas or you'll have an accident!'

Breaking was a procedure that Thomas hadn't quite mastered, so the alternative was to drag both feet hard along the ground. It had the same effect as disc brakes on a car and brought the bike to a fairly rapid halt. At that moment, Thomas imagined he heard his mum's voice...'How do you manage to wear out your shoes so quickly?' But, until he could master the brakes there was no real answer to that question.

Scooting along the lane with no restriction on the speed, Thomas' arrival home was quicker than usual. He propped the bike against the wall to cries of 'Thomas put that bike away,' which he ignored and, after waiting impatiently for his grandmother to unlock the door, he danced into the room shouting, 'Hello Cat! Where are you?'

But when there was no reply, he couldn't hide his disappointment, especially after such an exciting bike ride home. He expected at least a meow or Cat to jump onto his lap.

'Cat is over the fields,' said Frances, 'so let's get on with tea and your homework.'

His disappointment didn't give him the energy to resist so, sitting at the table, he slumped down like a rag doll.

'Come on Thomas, Cat will be back, so cheer up.' And with these words of comfort, he settled down to eat his tea.

Afterwards he started his homework - learning new words for a dreaded spelling test and reading from his book, something he usually enjoyed.

His mum came home from work and, seeing Thomas was feeling a bit down, she said 'Let's choose a name for Cat, because I think he has found a new home with us.'

Thomas thought this was a good idea and cheered up by chanting a list of his friends - Max, Ned, Zak and Alisha, a girl he was particularly fond of. In this happy frame of mind, both Mother and Grandmother decided to let the totally-unsuitable-naming continue unchecked.

'I think I'll go for a walk,' said Frances.

'Let me come with you and perhaps we'll meet Cat,' said Thomas.

'No, you stay here with your mum,' said his grandmother and, going out into the hall, she slipped her coat over her shoulders and closed the front door quietly behind her.

The wind was blowing around Frances' coat and she shivered when one gust caught her as she turned into the main road. With a quickening pace, and head down against the wind, she walked up the hill.

When a black and red splash in the grass verge caught her eye she gasped and realised that it was the body of Cat. Tears welled-up and rolled down her face. She had a lump in her throat and her sobs shook her body.

How could this have happened? To lose the little animal so soon after reluctantly letting it into their lives and enjoying the affection it demanded and gave? If it hadn't followed them home that night, it would probably be curled up asleep, safe and warm, somewhere right now instead of lying dead and frozen on the path beside her.

The sheer injustice epitomised in the body of Cat - killed by someone driving too fast or carelessly - was almost overwhelming.

How could they tell Thomas? What would they tell him?

Frances knelt down next to the body of Cat and, taking a plastic bag, she put Cat inside, returned home and quietly went round to the back of the house. She laid Cat on hay in the old, empty rabbit hutch out in the garden.

Mother and grandmother decided to tell Thomas that as Cat hadn't returned and it was most likely that she had gone back to her old home.

Em could hardly speak when she told him the white lie, but knew the truth would shatter his life. That Cat was missing was bad enough. It was the first time Thomas had grieved for the loss of a friend. He hadn't understood why Cat would want to leave him: she'd enjoyed living there, hadn't she, and he was her friend.

'Always remember that you loved Cat and that Cat loved you. And loving something that much is a great thing to do.'

The silence that followed seemed to last for an eternity before Frances, Em and Thomas hugged each other with just their tears for comfort.

Thomas broke away and, going over to the window, he opened it and cried, 'Cat you can come back here whenever you want. We love you.'

Cat's spirit was lying just a few feet away from Thomas...

'Thank you, Thomas. I will miss you too. Thank you for loving me the way you do. I will always rest near you.'

The Room

Jocelyn Edington

The party had been brilliant. Her friends Amy and Meg had brought her. She'd worn her new dress, a sparkling black number, and her new high-heeled ankle boots. He'd been a friend of the hostess, an elegant woman with silver hair. There had been some gossip associated with her and she tried to remember what it was. A younger lover? A high-profile divorcée with accusations of abuse?

Meg had pointed him out to her. A powder blue tuxedo, the colour of his eyes, an angular face and shiny white teeth. He was in-between girlfriends. She should go up to him. They were sure he was looking at her. She didn't out of shyness, but later and much drunker, when she went to the bar to refill her drink, he was there.

'Are you enjoying the party?' he asked. 'Or are you finding it a bore?'

'I love parties, even bad ones.'

He poured her a glass of wine.

'I'm starting to like it myself, now that I'm talking to the most beautiful woman in the room. Did anyone ever tell you your eyes are flecked with gold?'

'And did anyone ever tell you you're a very good talker?'

'Ah, but I mean every word. So you think I'm lying?'

She was finding herself attracted to him. He had moved closer to her and she could smell his cologne, woody with a trace of citrus. She fought the attraction and mustered some bravado.

'Absolutely. You're the type of man my mother warned me about.'

She stepped back, creating more space between them, but he moved towards her until their hips were touching. The sensation was electric.

'Who are you anyway?'

'Oh, just one of the Rothschilds. The Baron and I, well I am a Duke you know, worth millions, you really should take up with me.'

She laughed.

'Is it really so obvious?'

'I'm afraid so. I can hear the New Jersey twang in your voice.'

'That is cruel.'

'There's nothing wrong with being from New Jersey. Some of my best friends are from there.'

He slipped his arm around her waist. 'You and I should go somewhere and get to know each other better.'

Later that night, in her alcoholic haze, she'd been impressed with the long driveway lined with trees and the old mansion, partially hidden in the shadows. He'd driven round to the back of the house where they'd had to traverse a stretch of wet lawn, ruining her shoes.

'Who lives here?'

'No one. A friend left me the key but they never come here. No one knows about it, just you and me.

That's why I parked at the back.' He kissed her and they almost didn't see the pool. He guided her away from the edge.

'If I fall in,' he said, 'you'll have to rescue me. I've never learned how to swim.'

She giggled and gave him a playful nudge. His whole body tensed and his fingers dug into her arm.

'I'm not joking.'

She felt herself blush and was glad he couldn't see her face in the dark. Inside, he lit a fire and opened a bottle of champagne. He couldn't have been a kinder, more sensitive lover. She hadn't once felt even a twinge of anxiety on her usually dependable radar.

The bedroom was cold. She shivered in her underwear. Below she could see a corner of the pool that sparkled in the morning sun giving the illusion of warmth. She tried the door again. It was locked from the outside, strange for a bedroom. But he'd be back soon. If only she had brought her phone into the bedroom last night. If only her clothes weren't scattered on the floor downstairs. If only she hadn't left the party with him.

But there was no reason to panic. It must have been a mistake. He'd accidentally locked the door when he left. To go where? To get her breakfast perhaps, a tray of toast and hot coffee, a glass of orange juice. She would have given a lot for something to drink. Her mouth felt like a desert; the alcohol had sapped all the moisture from her body.

It was then she started to feel a sense of dread.

What if he wasn't coming back?

The bedroom was three stories up, no balconies or parapets to disrupt the smooth façade. She thought of tying sheets together and breaking the windows but they were solidly barred. She could break the windows and call for help but the place seemed deserted and the winter wind would blow in. If there had been heat but the room was stone cold and only the lights worked. She wrapped a musty blanket around her shoulders and took up her position at the door, calling and then shouting into the cracks.

The pale winter sun came and went. She went back to the bed and crawled under the blankets, her fingers raw and bleeding now from trying to pry open the door, her hands full of splinters from bashing the chair against it. All futile. Her throat was parched and hope was ebbing away. She heard a noise and stumbled to the window, but there was no one. Then she looked down to the corner of the pool visible from her window. There was something in the water. It floated to the edge, a body, face down, in a blue tuxedo. She let out a silent scream.

The Great Fire of Bédar

MarianMay Simpson

Hot days, dry shrub, dead grass,
an oven baked wind, an innocent spark
kindles and bursts into flames.
Changing winds fan the blaze ever bigger,
leaping roads uncontrolled, the villagers unaware.
A bright red glow,
creeping brown smoke and the village takes notice,
alert your friends, take care.
Roaring flames consume pine trees in seconds,
winds change.
Volcano-like rivers leave the ground
a festering red.
Get out, Get out, Grab what you can,
Don' t Panic, Don' t Panic,
where' s the car?
There 's the dog,
Oh my God where 's the cat?
I'm not going 'till he comes back.
Boil up some chicken and he'll come home,
Guardia not amused, tries to order us out.

Close off the roads, you cannot go home.

By dusk the monster is over the hill,
skirting the village,
heading south.
The raging inferno scorching a trail,
spreading fast,
fiercely hot,
hard to control.
Helicopters, like storks with their bundles,
drop water bombs filled from the sea.

Close off the roads, you cannot go home.

Village bars, now safe from the flames, give shelter
to yesterday's merrymakers now huddled in fear.
What have I lost?
Am I insured?
They wait and watch,
chaos, screaming sirens, the frightening noise.
Darkness falls,
the work is not done,
the angry red mass holding on.
Sightless birds in the sky stop dumping their loads,
as the men on the ground continue to fight.

Close off the roads, you dare not go home.

By morning the fire is losing its hold,
the fried black mess beginning to settle.
The country is bare now,
dry as a tinder box with ash in the air.

Open the roads, now you can go home.

Smouldering ground and blackened twigs.
Trees, headless skeletons,
all withered and roasted.
Melted cables on poles hung like washing lines,
clothesless,
scorched,
toasted.
White houses now blackened by smoke,
their windows have burst.
A blanket of ash for a terrace,
red soup for a pool.

Roads are open, you are home now.

Neighbourhood Watch

Lyn McCulloch

(First published in *The Lady*).

'I think it was the telescope that did it,' Maureen explained to her friend Sheila over tapas on the terrace. 'Everyone has binoculars, but the telescope was just too much.'

Sheila sipped her Rioja and chose her words carefully. 'I think people found it a bit spooky. Knowing that Gerald was up here spying on them.'

'He didn't mean any harm.' Maureen raised a hanky to her right eye and wiped away the start of a tear.

'I know love, but you know what people are like here on the *Campo*.' They lapsed into silence, looking out over the sun-drenched *Campo de Cortijo*, or Ex-pats' Hill, as it was more commonly known. Dotted with white or ochre villas, each in its own plot with swimming pool and terraces on all sides to follow the sun, the hill stood across the valley from Cassita, a traditional white Spanish village. Below, on either side of a rock-strewn, dry riverbed, orange trees and an olive grove fought for survival in the pale, arid earth. A dog barked in the distance and a couple of hundred yards away a blue saloon car could be seen bumping up the track towards a particularly impressive dwelling.

'Ralph's off up to Verena's again, I see.' Sheila looked around but Maureen shook her head.

'I've put the binoculars away. It doesn't seem appropriate somehow. Disrespectful, you know?'

'I suppose so.' Sheila picked some rosemary from a bush, which flourished in a pot on the terrace, rubbed it and sniffed. 'Maureen, you don't really think Ralph had anything to do with it do you? I know he was angry after the party but…'

Maureen sighed. 'I don't know. The police can't tell. Either Gerald just ran off the road, not concentrating, or maybe headlights or something blinded him. They interviewed Ralph, but then they also talked to Hans and Helga from La Bodega and Graham too. We'll just never know.'

'Hans and Helga?' They both looked across at a Moorish villa with turrets and a dome. 'What do they know?'

'Probably nothing,' said Maureen.

Despite the sun, Sheila shivered. 'It's the idea of someone in the community being involved. You know, someone from the hill.'

'I have to tell myself it was an accident.' Maureen reached for her wine and sighed.

Sheila took her hand. 'I'm sorry, I shouldn't talk about it.'

'No, it's all right. It's just a bit raw still. Oh, how I wish we'd never had that wretched lunch party!'

Everything had been ready and on the dot of twelve, Gerald put his eye to the telescope, recently mounted on the south terrace, and took a sweeping look across the hill.

'Sheila's just bringing in her washing. I guess she'll be a bit late.' He looked further up the hill. 'Hans is getting the car out so he and Helga will be here in a minute. Ralph – oh, Ralph's just arrived at Verena's. Are they actually going to be brave enough to arrive together do you think? Admit to us all that they're 'an item' as they say these days?'

'I shouldn't think so. Oh, Gerald, come away.' Maureen, embarrassed at her husband's nosiness, bent to pull a weed from one of the cluster of glazed pots, carefully placed to add colour to the terrace.

He swung the telescope up towards the villa above them and said, 'I wonder why Graham's not coming. He's in. I can see him up on his roof.'

Maureen busied herself arranging a tray of Serrano ham and olives. 'Perhaps he just didn't fancy another party.' She helped herself to a sliver of Manchego cheese. 'There have been quite a few lately.'

Gerald snorted. 'I think it's just plain unsociable. Particularly when you've been so helpful to him, doing his accounts and all that.'

The discussion stopped as Hans and Helga drew up in their red jeep. Maureen and Gerald lapsed easily into hospitality mode. They'd done a lot of entertaining before Gerald retired from the Bank and it was second nature to them.

Guests arrived, some by car and some on foot. It was always the same crowd, plus or minus a few. They gathered regularly on one terrace or another and were easy in each other's company.

The wine flowed and Maureen glanced over at Gerald, flushed and sweating slightly as he re-filled his glass. He was drinking too much these days. It was the ex-pat curse. Too much time and inexpensive booze was a poor combination.

She looked over at Graham's villa, but there was nothing to see.

Ralph had arrived separately from Verena but there were still a few glances. They'd been the talk of the *Campo* for weeks and most people were sure there was 'something going on'. Verena was divorced and Ralph's wife had recently left him for the local swimming pool engineer, and tongues were wagging furiously.

'So,' Ralph hailed Gerald, 'this is the new toy then?'

'Certainly is. Do you want to have a look.'

Ralph bent and put his eye to the lens. 'Hey Verena, it's trained straight on to your terrace.'

Verena stiffened and the smoked salmon parcel in her hand hovered just inches from her lips. 'My terrace! Why?'

'Oh, pure coincidence.' Gerald gestured expansively across the hill. 'I sweep round every so often just to see what everyone's up to.' Maureen knew he was joking, even though it was true, but as she looked round she realised one or two people weren't happy.

'Hey!' Ralph's tone was light, but his expression grim. 'That's a bit over the top. Binoculars is one thing, but a telescope!'

Maureen stepped in. 'He's only joking, Ralph. We use it to watch the stars. It's brilliant down here. None of the light pollution we used to have at home. There was a fantastic meteor shower the

43

other night, wasn't there, Gerald?'

But Gerald's wine consumption had robbed him of his usual ability to read a situation and react accordingly. 'Stars are okay, but the activity on this hill is enough to keep me busy! Nobody moves without it being noted here.'

Maureen tried to defuse what was rapidly becoming a nightmare. 'Oh, really, Gerald. That's not true!'

But he wasn't even listening any more. 'Look!' He swung the telescope round and pointed at Graham's villa. 'There he is, up on his roof when he should be down here joining in the fun. Unsociable git.'

Maureen laughed, a high, brittle sound, but it was too late; one by one the assembled company made their excuses and left until only Sheila, up to her elbows in suds, washing glasses, remained.

'You damned fool, Gerald!' Maureen was furious with him. 'Now look what you've done. Everybody thinks you spend all day watching their every move.'

'Well! Actually I do.' Gerald was pouring a whisky. 'You wouldn't believe some of the goings-on I can see from here. I'll tell you what, Sheila,' he said, as he meandered into the kitchen, 'don't let anyone tell you there's nothing going on between Ralph and Verena. I've seen what goes on up on her roof terrace.'

'Gerald.' Sheila dried her hands and reached for her handbag. 'I really don't want to know. I'm off.' She kissed Maureen and left abruptly.

It was two nights later that Gerald met with his accident. He was driving home, hurrying to get back in time for the annual Cassita Bowls Club Dinner, when his car veered from the road, landing upside-down in the scrubland below. By the time anyone realised what had happened it was too late. As Maureen explained, she thought he'd gone directly to the dinner so she didn't raise the alarm till after midnight.

Hans reported that he'd been on his terrace with binoculars, trying to identify a particularly unusual bat that was skimming his swimming pool, when he'd seen a very powerful flash of light. Whatever it was, the police believed it could have blinded Gerald at just the wrong moment causing him to lose control.

Someone told the police about the party and the telescope conversation and they started snooping round asking questions. Apart from the occasional burglary there was little contact between the Spanish police and the folk on the hill and the Guardia had trouble working out the dynamics of the ex-pat community. After only a few days, the local Chief of Police had arrived on Maureen's doorstep, shrugged in a very Mediterranean way and told her that there was no proof it was anything other than an accident. She had to believe him.

The funeral was well attended. They knew a lot of people in the area and, until that last party, had always been a popular couple. At the gathering afterwards, the cover was firmly over the telescope which stood, like an extra guest, on the terrace.

Sheila threw back the last of her wine and peered at her watch in the gathering gloom. 'I can't believe I've sat here all afternoon!'

'I'm glad. I've enjoyed having you. Gerald may not have been the world's most exciting companion but it's odd how I miss him now he's gone.'

'Still,' Sheila struggled out of the deep padded chair, 'better make a move. I've had a few though. Can I leave the car here and I'll stroll over for it in the morning?'

'Fine.'

'I'll need a torch. If I try and do it without one in this light I'll fall into those ruts in the track.'

'Sure, hang on. I'll go and find one.'

Maureen headed for the hall cupboard and reached for the big, powerful, yellow searchlight that sat on the shelf. It was heavy and as she took it down she had second thoughts. Perhaps not. Next to it was a little, black, rubber torch and she reached for that and gave it to Sheila to guide her home.

She watched the feeble beam of light wobbling up the track in the dark. Once she'd seen Sheila safely onto her own ground, she went to the kitchen for a black rubbish sack. She took the searchlight down and wrapped it carefully, making a mental note to put it in the big bin in town next time she was there. Silly to keep it.

Back on the terrace she looked up at the villa above, where a light shone in the window. She went to the 'phone and dialled a number from memory. 'Hi, darling. It's me. Are you coming down?'

'Count to sixty and I'll be there.'

The light went out in Graham's sitting room and moments later he stood on the terrace, a bottle of wine in his hand. Together they walked inside and drew the curtains.

Maureen turned on a couple of table lamps and put a match to the fire, already laid in the grate. 'Isn't it nice to be able to do this?' she commented, settling on the sofa in his arms. 'Just you and me.'

A Fare Warning

Jane Breay

He sat in his car, as he had the first Saturday of every month for nearly three years, watching the youngsters as they piled out of the bars and clubs, mostly worse for wear. There were so many cities, so many streets, so many clubs. He could do this for a hundred years and never visit the same place twice.

He had parked a little way from the bright lights to make it harder to identify the logo on his door. It was taking longer than usual tonight but however anxious he felt, he would not allow his nerves to push him into breaking his cardinal rule: it had to be someone on her own.

It was nearly 3am before his patience was rewarded. A gaggle of girls came staggering out of a club. One waved goodbye to the rest and stood unsteadily at the kerbside, scanning the wet street for a taxi. He cruised gently up, opening the passenger window as he drew level. He was a good mimic and tonight adopted the local Yorkshire accent.

'Need a cab, luv?'

'Err. Yeah, I s'pose so.' She peered drunkenly at the cab logo, and he leaned across to unlatch the door. That simple gesture encouraged them into the passenger seat, which made the job so much easier.

'Best get in if you don't want to get soaked.'

She pulled the door fully open and almost fell in.

'Where to?'

She mumbled an address and slumped down into the seat.

'You need to fasten your seat belt.'

'What … oh, yeah.' He waited as she fumbled the belt into its slot before he moved off.

Her head lolled to the right and her eyes were closed, allowing him to study her in the glow of the streetlights as he drove. She was pretty enough beneath all that make-up, but her style of dress was designed to attract the wrong sort of attention, just like so many of them, even the brightest and most sensible. Another potential fashion victim in the truest sense of the word.

He headed in the direction of the address she had given him and by the time he reached the end of her street she was snoring gently. He carried on past – no need to abort the plan this evening.

Another mile and they were out of the built-up area. He turned off the main road into a country lane and pulled up after a hundred yards, beside a wood.

She was still sleeping soundly and he had no difficulty handcuffing her wrists and was tying her ankles before she woke.

'Hey, where are we? What're you doing?' She struggled to sit upright, glaring at him and he could see terror sobering her up faster than a cold shower.

He finished knotting the rope round her ankles and watched her in silence as she struggled and shouted 'Help!!' several times.

'You can scream all you like, but no one's going to come. I've sat here most of the night for a whole week without seeing anyone.'

He closed the passenger door and walked far enough down the lane to be out of sight. He took out a receiver the size of a mobile and switched it on to listen to the sounds from the car. He knew he would need to wait at least five minutes until the frantic shouts subsided into sobs and finally to sniffles. The wait was part of the ritual. He needed her properly scared before the next phase and that meant giving her time to think through the worst possibilities. He knew it would work better if she thought he had abandoned her.

Returning to the car he saw that her hair was dishevelled and huge tears were running down her face in tracks of mascara. Her eyes pleaded with him and she looked utterly beaten.

'What are you going to do with me?' she asked in a squeaky whisper.

'What d'you think?'

'I…I… don't know… rape me? … kill me?' she stammered, 'Please don't, please just let me go. I won't tell anyone, not even my parents. I won't contact the police… please.'

Always the same pleas. It was difficult not to show how they affected him, but they were an important part of the ritual.

He continued with the well-rehearsed speech.

'Yes. You may not be far from home but you might as well be a hundred miles. I could drag you into that wood and do whatever I fancy and leave you to find your way home. Or I could kill you and bury you and who knows if you'd ever be found.'

He watched her in silence for several more seconds as she stared at him, her eyes wide with fear as yet more tears coursed down her cheeks, creating two big black stains on the collar of her pink jacket.

Finally, he decided she was ready.

He switched on the interior light and picked a photo off the top of the dashboard. He angled it so that she had a good view of a pretty girl of about twenty sitting on a beach, smiling at the camera. She had long auburn curls, green eyes and a dazzling smile.

He maintained the Yorkshire accent but deliberately softened it to a more educated tone.

'This is my daughter, Julie. She was a medical student. It's all she ever wanted after we lost her mum to cancer. She was bright, funny, caring and beautiful inside and out. She was my best friend and the focus of my whole life for nearly ten years.

'She worked hard, but she liked to play too. One night four years ago she went out to celebrate the end of her exams and did what you just did. She separated from her friends and got into an unlicensed cab.'

'He drove her down a country lane, beat her, raped her and left her for dead. She was found alive and seemed to have completely recovered.

'They had enough evidence to make the charges stick when they finally caught him. Then a month before the trial she died of a brain haemorrhage, caused by the beating.' He paused, staring through the windscreen, allowing his own tears to flow but fighting the catch in his voice.

'No one can replace her and nothing can ever bring her back. But if I can stop it happening to just one more girl, I know she would approve and it gives me a reason to live.'

He turned to look at her, his eyes seeking her forgiveness.

'I hope you understand now that I mean you no harm. Quite the opposite. I'm truly sorry I had to frighten you but I've found that it really is the best way of getting the message across.

'Julie was an intelligent, sensible girl. She knew the rules but she broke them and we both paid a terrible price.'

He examined her face closely and was satisfied that the terror was subsiding, although the tension still showed in her hunched shoulders.

'I'm going to take you home soon, I promise.

'Do I need to leave the cuffs on until we get nearer to your house? I don't want you running off and being picked up by someone who really *is* dangerous.' He smiled encouragingly.

She shook her head and he leaned over to cut the rope round her ankles. She offered her hands for him to remove the cuffs, the strain on her face gradually giving way to bewilderment.

'You might like to clean your face up a bit,' he said, passing her a pack of wipes and some tissues.

When she had finished he offered her a bottle of water and she sipped gratefully.

'Better now? '

She nodded and when she found her voice he was pleased that it was firm and confident.

'You've done this before?'

'Every month for more than three years. Always a different town. Always the first Saturday - Julie was taken on the first Saturday in June.

'Do you have any idea how many women are assaulted every year in unlicensed cabs?'

She shook her head.

'Far, far too many. At least one a week. Even those who live to tell the tale never really get over it.'

It was time to move onto the final phase. He needed her cooperation, which meant gaining her trust. He was pretty sure she no longer saw him as a threat but now he needed to achieve a degree of empathy.

He asked her about herself and after a moment's hesitation she told him that she was waiting for her A Level results and her grades were predicted to be good. She wanted to be a journalist.

Her shoulders relaxed and she smiled as she talked about her Yorkie who was always causing mayhem by running off.

When she reached the point where she was confident enough to ask him what he did, he knew they were nearly done.

'I used to teach IT at Julie's school. After she died I came close to a breakdown and I retired on grounds of ill health. I do a bit of consultancy, which gives me the flexibility to do this. It can take several days in a strange town to find a good isolated spot close enough to the centre.

'Ok to take you home now?'

'Yes, please.' She hesitated, then as the car moved off, 'I thought you looked far too nice to be a rapist or worse. You could be my dad – you even talk like him! But I guess the most ordinary-looking people can be evil.'

'That's exactly my point – murderers don't generally have 'avoid me at all costs' tattooed on their forehead.'

As they pulled up beside her house she fished in her bag for her purse and asked formally, 'What do I owe you?'

He smiled and shook his head.

'Just promise you'll spread the word among your friends. Tell them to use licensed cabs or pre-book a mini cab from a reputable firm. Plus, *never* get into the front seat.' He hesitated, waiting until he heard her say, 'I promise.'

'Picking you up like that could be construed as abduction, which could get me put away for several years.'

She nodded. 'I won't tell anyone. I promise, I really do. And I'm so very sorry about your daughter.'

She got out and walked up the path. As she turned to wave in the open doorway, he was gratified to see her smile shyly and mouth 'thank you.' He had definitely chosen well this time – a budding journalist would surely find a way to spread the word.

'Another good evening for Guardian Angel Cabs,' he said to himself as he pulled away. He glanced in the rear-view mirror. A familiar face, auburn curls glinting in the lamplight, smiled at him from the back seat and nodded her approval.

Ciao

Jean McGrane

'Please think carefully, Maria. You only have a week to change your mind.'

'OK Mama. I have to go now. Ciao Mama.'

'Ciao Bella.'

Maria replaced the phone heavily on its hook and leant her forehead against the yellowing wall of the corridor. Tears pricked behind her eyes as she imagined her mother in their bright kitchen in Napoli, turning to relay all the false optimism to her husband that she had just been fed by Maria. She sighed. There was no chance of a private conversation with her parents now that her mobile phone contract had been terminated. If she didn't have to shout over the clatter of the kitchen on the public phone, would she have told them more? Probably not.

'Maria. Come on. They're waiting for you,' Rodrigo called from the door to the bar.

'OK, OK, I'm coming.' She picked up her guitar case and followed him.

In the evenings, the posters of bullfighters, the sultry music and the dark corners of the bar were part of the atmosphere for couples choosing this unfashionable dockside area for their secret liaison. But in the daytime the spell was broken to reveal scuffed chairs, greasy tables and a sticky, beer-stained floor. This lunchtime there were only a handful of dock workers and sailors crouched over the bar drinking beer and eating tapas, a bored barman playing on a gaming machine and a couple of workmen in blue overalls sitting at a table eating the *menu del día*. The small band playing to themselves only seemed to emphasise the dismal scene.

Maria took her place and began to play; her head bent low over her guitar. Through the delicate plucking of the strings she breathed her homesickness: through the dramatic strums she vented her feelings of frustration. It was meant to have been so different. All she had wanted was to experience a world of music outside her native Italy. She had never intended to spend a year trapped in one single bar in a rough part of Barcelona.

She remembered her mother's fretful words from the phone call, 'But, Maria, I don't understand. You have had your year away from your studies. You have learned the classical style of music that you wanted. Now your place at the University is waiting for you and the term starts next week – and yet you still don't come home.'

How could she tell them; disappoint them?

As she lost herself in the music, her mood changed from self-pity into feelings of anger. She remembered the first time she had heard Antonio play his guitar in that same bar in her first week away from home on her grand adventure. She had been moved to tears; transported by his passion. And in the days and weeks that followed, as he had taught her to play, her passion for the music had spilled over into a passion for Antonio – a passion that had lasted for almost a year. But this morning she had returned from the shops with bread and milk to find that he was gone, leaving only crumpled sheets and the smell of his cheap cologne.

When she had left the room to come to the bar at lunchtime, the landlord had accosted her.

'*Señorita*, a word with you please. I must ask you for the rent money. It hasn't been paid for a month now and you owe me 500 euros.'

Maria had stared at him in disbelief. 'I don't understand. I gave Antonio my share of the rent every week. I understood he was paying you.'

'You are mistaken. When *Señor* Antonio left this morning he told me that you would be paying the bill for the room.'

'But I haven't got that sort of money. It's Antonio that you should be asking for the money.'

'*Señor* Antonio has gone. If you can't pay, then I will have to call the Guardia.'

'No, please. Give me a little time. Perhaps I can get the money.'

'I'll give you two days but in the meantime I must insist that you give me your passport as security.'

Maria had been forced to hand over her passport and, despite a phone call to her parents, in the end she had been too ashamed to ask them for money.

Maria sighed heavily. She had to admit that despite the initial shock of finding Antonio gone, it was not altogether unexpected and she realised that, now that it had happened, she was beginning to feel the warm beginnings of relief. The romance with Antonio – and with this life - had been over months ago and she saw with a new clarity that it was time to go home and build a different future. Her despair was not for Antonio but that she had no money for a flight home. Even if she could sneak out of the room without paying the landlord, she couldn't get back to Italy without her passport. She was trapped.

The music was over but Maria's head was still bowed over her guitar as she allowed her tears to course down her cheeks. She gradually became aware of someone close to her, clapping enthusiastically. She lifted her head.

'That was brilliant. So very, very good.'

Maria, deep in her despair, stared unseeing at the young man standing next to her.

'Hi! I'm Patrick.' A tall fresh-faced boy put out his hand to shake hers. 'I'm a guitarist myself - straightforward R&B, nothing like you play. I would just love to learn to play classical Spanish guitar.'

'Maria. My name is Maria,' she said flatly, taking his hand and smiling a little at the formal gesture.

'Great. Can I buy you a drink, Maria?'

Maria shrugged and they walked over to a table as the rest of the band packed up and left. Right now a little alcohol to take away the sharp edges of her despair seemed like a good idea.

'Patrick. Are you coming?' called his friends from the door.

'No. I think I'll hang on here for a while.'

'Well, don't be late. We have to be at Dock 4 at 5pm to go through security together.'

'OK. OK I'll be there,' he called back, already turning to Maria.

Over the course of several brandies Patrick told Maria how he was on a gap year, playing in a small band on a circuit of cruise ships sailing around the Mediterranean before beginning University.

'My parents want me to study accountancy but I just wanted to give it a go and see if I could make my living as a musician. Working on a cruise ship just wasn't the best way of doing it, I guess,' he said with a small shrug. Patrick picked up Maria's guitar, the one that had taken all her travel money to buy when she'd moved in with Antonio and had decided to stay.

Maria smiled quietly seeing the similarities between Patrick and the girl she had been a year ago: their naiveté and dreams. She ached for a chance to regain his level of enthusiasm and felt sadness for the certainty that it would be crushed in him as it had been in her.

'Here, let me show you,' she said kindly as she corrected the shaping of his fingers on the frets.

As the afternoon wore on, she learned more from Patrick about his job on the cruise ship. 'It's not too bad – I'm getting to see some new places – or at least some bars in some new places,' he smiled weakly. 'We've been on a couple of different ships already. They don't pay a fortune but there's nowhere to spend money anyway so I'm saving quite a bit. We're joining a Saga cruise this afternoon and our first stop will be Naples. I've never been to Italy before.'

'Napoli. That's my home,' she said, suddenly coming alive.

'Really?' Patrick's speech was becoming more slurred with every brandy and his eyelids were drooping.

'We should change places – you and I, Patrick. You want to learn some real guitar and I want to get home.' But she couldn't be sure that Patrick had heard her as he mumbled something unintelligible and laid his head on the table.

'Maria,' Rodrigo called to her, 'We are waiting to close. Take your friend somewhere else.'

Maria started to protest, 'He's not my friend,' but Patrick looked so young that she couldn't see him just put out on the street.

'OK, OK. Just help me to get him on his feet.'

Together, Maria and Rodrigo pulled Patrick upright and Maria managed to walk him, leaning heavily on her, the few yards to her room further down the street where he slumped onto the bed, snoring.

'Great! This is all I need. The landlord won't be too happy about this cithcr.'

Maria glanced at her watch. With a jolt she saw that it was already 4.30pm. Patrick had to be on board his ship by 5pm.

She shook his shoulder roughly. 'Patrick, Patrick. Wake up. You will miss your boat sailing.'

But there was no response from Patrick beyond a mumble and a further snore.

Maria stood, looking down at the sleeping figure while an idea formed in her mind. It was an idea that both excited and appalled her. She looked at her watch again. There was no time to dither.

'Look Patrick, I don't know if you can hear me but this is what we are going to do. I am going back to Napoli to begin my University course and restart my life. And you are going to get away from playing for old ladies to waltz on cruise ships and give yourself a chance to learn some real guitar and to see the world.'

Maria hesitated for a long moment and then quickly reached into Patrick's pocket for his wallet and took out some notes.

She began to scribble on the back of an old envelope, 'Patrick, I've left you my guitar and taken 500 euros – that's half what I paid for it but it's just enough to cover my rent. If you want to rejoin your boat, your job will be waiting for you in Naples – I won't need it anymore. But Patrick, why don't you follow your dream? That's what I'm going to do. Maria.'

Maria snatched up the money and threw a few belongings in a bag. There was very little time. She was going to have to run all the way to the docks.

At the foot of the stairs, the landlord was waiting, blocking her exit. 'Your rent money, Señor,' Maria declared as she pushed the notes into his hand. 'And I will need my passport now please.'

The landlord looked at the money in his hand. 'How did you get this? Have you robbed someone?'

Maria winced. 'No, not robbed. It's none of your business but I've made a trade.' She tried to ignore

61

the smirk on his face as she snatched the passport from his hand. 'Now, if you will excuse me, I have somewhere I must be.' She began to walk towards the door with as much dignity as she could muster but at the last moment turned and added, 'Oh, and I think you have a new tenant.'

Maria strode out of the building and turned towards the docks but at the last minute, some instinct made her turn and look towards the window of the room where she had spent the last unforgettable months of her life. With a jolt, Maria saw that Patrick was standing at the window, rubbing his eyes and looking dazed - her note in his hand. She held her breath as their eyes met, then slowly opened the palms of her hands as if to ask for his agreement to the deal.

She watched as Patrick ran his hand through his tousled hair, looked down at the note again and, finally, turned his eyes on her and shrugged. Maria beamed a smile at him and blew a kiss. 'Ciao, Patrick,' she called as she turned and began to run towards the docks and her new life.

Albert Gets Married

Ian Patrick

*Adapted from The Lion and Albert
and its sequel Albert's Return
by Marriott Edgar.*

'Appen you've 'eard about Albert
Who was ate up by t'lion in t'cage?
Well, the lion didn't find Albert tasty
And spat Albert out in a rage.

Now Albert grew up and was courting
It gave Mam and Dad quite a turn,
'E'd never shown interest in women,
Facts of life 'ee still 'ad to learn.

One night Albert brought home his Jenny,
She wasn't a beauty 'tis true,
With 'air on 'er lip and big buck teeth
And a cross-eye she couldn't see through.

But Albert was ever so smitten,
In 'is eyes she was simply perfect,
'E said they'd be married in t'chapel,
With two bridesmaids, as you'd expect.

Now Mr and Mrs Ramsbottom
Asked them why they should wed in such
haste?
'Is there owt else that you should tell us?'
'Of course not,' said Albert, red faced.

'Ee by gum,' said 'is Mam in a panic,
'I'll need a new frock and an 'at.
And an 'andbag and shoes to go with it.'
Albert's Dad, in dumb horror, just sat.

'I suppose that it's one of them posh do's
Where I'll need a top 'at and a tie?
I'm not rightly fond of weddings
Since my own,' 'ee said, with a sigh.

Mam said, 'It's a long way to chapel.
I hope that we're going by car.
In new shoes, I'd soon be fair crippled
If I 'ad to walk very far.'

The day soon arrived, guests assembled,
Waiting for t'bride to appear.
The organ played while they were waiting
Whilst Albert stood there, looking queer.

The wedding music was playing
As Jenny walked down the aisle.
She seemed in a very big hurry, but
'Er eyes shone and she 'ad a big smile.

The preacher asked them both, 'Will you?'
Jenny said, very quickly, 'I will.'
Albert stood there looking uncertain
Until prompted by 'er brother, Bill.

The reception was in t'social club back room,
Which was cheaper than t'pub down the street.
They 'ad sandwiches, pork pies and pickles
And all different dishes of meat.

They toasted the couple with champagne
Bought from Asda - a pint was ten pound.
Albert thought that it tasted like cider,
There was more than enough to go round.

They were going to Spain for their honeymoon,
Where they hoped they'd get lots of sunshine.
Albert's mother said, 'we went to Southport
And we couldn't care less if t'were fine.'

That was too much information for Albert,
'E knew that she'd been on the gin.
'E said to his new wife,
''Ope Dad don't get drunk,
Or then fun and games would begin.'

They got on the plane, they were nervous,
They'd not flown before and that's true.
Albert said 'e wished that they'd travelled by boat,
And Jenny agreed with him too.

Finally, the aeroplane landed.
Their honeymoon, at last, 'ad begun.
I won't bore you recounting the details.
Just to say that, that night they 'ad fun.

Well Albert 'ad seemingly excelled.
At long last, 'ee'd got something right.
Nine months later almost to the day,
Their new son came into sight.

'By gum, 'e looks just like Albert.
'E sounds just like our Albert too.
But one thing that we're going to tell Albert,
Is to keep 'im away from the zoo!'

The Verdict

Doug Day

There was a buzz of activity in Court 1. The jury had agreed on a verdict and were coming back into court after four days of deliberation.

This was a scene that Detective Superintendent David Ashcroft had witnessed regularly during almost thirty years of police service. He watched the lead barristers, wigs in hand, rushing to their benches, trailed by their juniors bending under the weight of the files resting in their arms. Members of the press were pushing and shoving to get onto the allocated benches. It was obvious that there were too many for the available space, but that didn't stop them trying to get colleagues to squeeze up a little more. Upstairs in the Public Gallery it was noisy and people could be heard climbing the stairs - each footfall sounding out on the solid wood flooring. These spectators peered down onto the court below as if at the theatre – indeed, many have likened court hearings to pure pieces of theatre.

The Courtroom dated from Georgian times. It was clearly built to intimidate and emphasise the power of justice and many a wretch had been sentenced to death within its four walls. The court was completely panelled with dark wood. An ornate white plastered vaulted ceiling, complete with skylight tower, provided the only natural light, and old candleholders around the room had been converted to electric and provided artificial light which was needed continuously.

The Judge's chair dominated the room. It was set above the rest of the court so the Judge could look down on participants. Directly above the red padded high chair rested the Royal Coat of Arms and, in front of the chair, there was a large fitted desk with the now unavoidable PC monitor and keyboard. At the next level down, the Clerk of the Court sat in front of the Judge and, on the main floor, were the legal benches. In front of the Judge's chair, and behind the legal benches, was the dock, set on its own and directly connected by stairs to the cells beneath. The jury was seated on three rows of benches to the right of the Judge's chair and opposite the witness box.

Each part had its own entrance so that no one came into direct contact with anyone else.

Superintendent Ashcroft looked across at Clayton Sweeney, a criminal with an unblemished record, never found guilty despite damning evidence. Witnesses always changed stories or were never seen again; jurors were intimidated or bought with enough money to pay off their mortgage or other debts. Sweeney and his team had been responsible for murder, theft, arson, money laundering, sex trade and, of course, drugs. Theirs was a huge empire, able to launder money through legitimate business interests.

And with money comes power.

Sweeney was feted by politicians, charities and indeed the legal profession - both the judiciary and police officers. That power had paid for the finest legal teams who had been able to pick through the evidence, looking for loopholes in procedures, and checking the background of witnesses. And when the dirty linen had been unearthed, the pressure was applied and the juror 'turned'.

Either way, this was to be Ashcroft's last case. He had spent the last fifteen years trying to bring Sweeney to justice. He'd seen trials collapse and juries return verdicts that were clearly wrong. Senior police officers and even the Crown Prosecution Service seemed reluctant to appeal against the verdicts and ask for a retrial.

Sweeney returned his stare and then smiled at Ashcroft. He seemed so confident of the outcome.

The jury was made up of seven men and five women. The average age seemed to be mid-forties and the only concession to youth was one of each sex, who looked about eighteen. An usher opened the door to the jury room. He directed them to the benches and to the seat each had used throughout the six-week trial. Many continued to inspect a pile of papers that contained notes, key points and documentary evidence. It was too late now, of course. A verdict had been reached. Perhaps, then, they were using the papers to shield them from the gaze of others in the court.

Superintendent Ashcroft studied the faces of the jurors, hoping to pick up an indication of the verdict. The clerk of the court entered through the door directly behind the Judge's chair and took his seat. He made eye contact with the barristers and nodded. Whether this was a greeting or confirmation of a verdict it was not possible to say.

Total quiet descended on the room and the door behind the Judge's chair opened.

An usher came from behind the chair, surveyed the room and, in a well-rehearsed and clear voice he announced, 'All rise.'

When the noise of people getting to their feet had abated, Judge Cosgrave entered his court wearing his purple robe with red sash and powdered wig. He bowed to the legal teams and the jury, and then took his seat.

The Clerk of the Court turned to the jury. 'Can the jury foreman please stand?'

With this, a bespectacled, grey-haired gentleman stood.

The Clerk looked at him. 'Have you reached a verdict on all the indictments listed?'

The foreman answered in a firm, clear voice, 'Yes.'

An audible murmur went round the court. Reporters had pens in hand, poised. People in the front row of the public gallery lent forward as far as possible to make sure they missed nothing of the drama that was about to unfold.

'On Count One - *Perverting the Course of Justice* - do you find the defendant guilty or not guilty?'

'Guilty.'

'Is that the verdict of you all?'

'Yes.'

Detective Superintendent Ashcroft raised his eyes towards the ceiling.

Guilty, after all this time.

He didn't know what to think.

The Clerk continued through several other indictments. Most were 'guilty' verdicts. Some not.

Judge Cosgrave was forced to silence the hubbub coming from the public gallery and threatened to clear the court and then, when all was quiet, he spoke...

'You have been found guilty of perverting the course of justice. Justice is the mark of a good and honest society. In your position you have shown a disregard to the rules of society. It gives me no pleasure to pass sentence, but in order to take stock, sentencing will be postponed for one week. You will, therefore, be remanded in custody. Take him down.'

It was Detective Superintendent Ashcroft who felt a hand on his shoulder and, as he turned to walk down the steps to the cells below the court, he heard loud cheers from the public gallery.

Now 'former' Detective Superintendent Ashcroft took one last look around the courtroom.

He looked at Sweeney.

Sweeney looked back at him. He had a smile on his face. It was a smile that faded quickly and turned to pure hatred. He pulled his forefinger across his throat and Ashcroft knew that 'contracts' would be taken out and he'd be lucky if he survived long enough in prison to hear his sentence.

Ashcroft descended the steps to the cells beneath.

He thought about the Jury.

What did any of them know about crime and criminals?

They'd return to their cosy lives and forget about the verdict in a couple of weeks.

And Sweeney?

He'd grow more and more powerful and would soon be 'untouchable'.

The Stranger

Linda Burton-Cooper

It was late June and the heat was unusually intense for early summer. It scorched down on all, leaving everything in its midst bleached and faded.

Taking shade under the canopy outside the bar, slumped in a chair I sipped my cooling beer.

'Who is that coming up the hill?' asked Pedro the patron, whilst casting a *tapa* of cheese onto my table.

Overheated and irritable, waving away the pestering flies, the only reply I could muster up was, 'don't know and I didn`t particularly care.' Shielding my eyes from the sun's glare, I curiously watched the black convertible Cadillac coming up the steep incline to the village, its V8 engine roaring with a fanfare of power.

Seated watchfully in a makeshift shebeen hidden inside an unused bus shelter were a group of local males lethargically drinking beer and playing cards. From their vantage point they could oversee all the comings and goings to the village. Alerted by the noisy engine they craned their necks to find its source, mouths dropping open, eyes bemused, they followed the vehicles assent.

A stranger!

A bristled look shot around the group.

Under watchful eyes, the driver expertly manoeuvred the convertible into a shaded spot outside the dilapidated *Hostal.*

The car door swung open and out stepped a black boot onto the tarmac, its owner, a tall crow like figure, straightened with fluid ease from the red leather car seat. The stranger's lank jet hair hung below a wide rimmed black Stetson. Standing boldly on the kerb he eyed all with an intensity that seemed to satisfy him that nothing had escaped his scrutiny. Apart from me.

Furtively, I leant back unseen into the canopy's shadow. This man was no stranger to me. I knew much of him, of his whole lineage, from *El Barrio*, a district in my native Madrid.

And I knew why he, Ronaldo Magus, was here!

Audible mumblings, accompanied by frantic fanning, caused a stir in the street as a group of widows walked by. The only relief to the mass of black clad activity were the flashes of colour from the flowers the women carried to adorn the graves of lost loved ones in the nearby cemetery.

'Buenos Días Señoras,' (good day ladies) the visitor's charming yet challenging voice called out. The group stopped abruptly and stared at the intruder distrustfully. Their leader replied haughtily *'Buenos Días'* and led the group scuttling off to where their dead waited.

The visitor nodded with a thin smile as if agreeing with himself that he had the measure of the village. Leaning into his black convertible he hoisted out a large leather holdall, swung it over his broad shoulder and pushed through the *Hostal's* front door.

'Well, tell me, who is he, you seemed to know him?' Pedro's impatient voice inquired.

74

'Have you not seen the posters bill boarded around?' I asked flatly. 'He is *The Magician*. He has come to entertain the children.'

'Huh, entertain the children? Frighten the life out of them, more like.' He snorted, cleaning the grey zinc table with a grubby cloth.

A familiar voice called from the back of the bar, 'Pedro! Quick, come here!' And Pedro sloped off obediently to the command of his vinegary wife.

Content with my bachelorhood and glad to be left alone I relaxed into a heat and beer-induced stupor, my mind wandering back to my youth and life in *The Barrio - my Barrio -* and the collection of characters one would meet daily in the streets and bars…

It was a cosmopolitan Barrio that embraced all and sundry, there was corruption and theft, extortion, whoring, murder, drug dealing, also laughter, camaraderie and love, but most of all the cohesive family networks that held people and business together.

One significant, I would dare say infamous family, was the Magus family. Magicians, said to have originated from southern Italy with a history of magic that went back centuries. They were known for their perfidious ways, no one was ever sure of what they had done or what they were capable of and, being foreigners, they held their own council and were generally feared.

Ronaldo was the youngest of the five Magus boys and was said to be the most formidable and disarmingly charming. Unlike his brothers, he spent some of his youth as an apprentice in Italy with the extended Magus family. Rumour was that he had got himself into a spot of trouble and was forced to return to Spain.

Some years back Ronaldo had become the gossip of The Barrio when his beautiful wife Sofia disappeared. My friend Sebastian was working as a stagehand on that fateful evening, when at the end of one of Ronaldo's popular magic shows Sofia did not appear for the final curtain call. In truth, she was never seen again after a staged disappearing act. Ronaldo had closed the velvet cubicle curtain on her smiling face and when he reopened it she was no longer there and in her place was a fluffy white rabbit wearing her Diamante necklace. The rabbit was proudly shown to an amazed audience who were cooing at the sight of the cuddly creature; having completely forgotten about the Magician's beautiful assistant

After the performance they searched everywhere. Her changing room was untouched; their home was as before. Nothing had been removed. It was as though she had magically disappeared into thin air.

For myself, I'd only ever seen the beautiful Sofia in posters. She was portrayed as a charismatic figure with a mane of thick hair. My stagehand friend Sebastian had assisted with their illusionist performances nightly at the theatre and knew her well.

He often talked about her 'a rare beauty, and the most bewitching woman I have ever seen, with a rich cascade of auburn hair, dancing green eyes who skips across the stage like a sprite. Ronaldo is a very lucky man,' he would say, as he swallowed down his brandy and unrequited love.

But perhaps Sebastian was not the only man besotted by the beautiful Sofia.

Sebastian and I would often sit in our local bar late into the night talking of his experiences working in the theatre. How, although setting up magical acts, he never ever quite knew how Ronaldo did his illusionist tricks. After a bottle of wine or two he would say knowingly 'there is magic beyond human consciousness. You know that don`t you?' I always agreed, knowing, from experience, that there was always more to life than met the eye.

Working in the theatre he did see and overhear many things, including the secretive conversations between the beautiful Sofia and Armando, Ronaldo`s assistant from Venezuela.

Not surprisingly, when Sofia disappeared, so did Armando, and neither were ever seen again.

It was believed that they had run off together whilst the magician was distracted, giving his extravagant bows and smiles to an appreciative audience at the end of the show.

The suspected affair between Sofia and Armando had become common knowledge and gossip was rife, and although the police warily interviewed Ronaldo and the Magus family, the matter was not pursued.

It was agreed by all in The Barrio, that he had been blinded by love and refused to admit to the affair between the lovers. But their eyes belied their true feelings and somehow, deep down, it was

*believed that Ronaldo had murdered them both and
had used devious magic to dispose of their bodies...*

Dusk was gently creeping in. It was a balmy
summer evening and the town hall square was filled
with plastic seats all focussed on the wooden plinth
stage where *The Magnificent Ronaldo* was to
perform his magic that evening. The Mayor stood in
the distance proudly watching the children excitedly
hogging the front rows, jumping up and down
anticipating the magician arrival at any moment.

Everyone started to clap as a local volunteer
hoisted up the curtain and stumbled across the stage
and tied it clumsily to the adjacent frame. *'Muy Bien
Juanito,'* (Very good Little John) called out a jovial
man standing in the wings. The audience clapped
enthusiastically and Juanito flushed, smiled and
bobbed a cursory bow before scooting off.

Suddenly, there was a short drum roll and thick
grey clouds of smoke enveloped the stage. And out
of its shadow emerged a dark flowing figure.

'Look there's a big bat,' cried out one of the
children in fear.

A shudder went through the crowd of watchers.
Now, at the front of the stage, stood the magician.
His cape bellowed open and out came black gloved
hands holding fluttering crow-like birds but before
anyone could adjust their eyes to the sight the
Magician fiercely clapped his hands together like
cymbals and the birds were no longer, just a shower
of tiny pieces of sooted paper that he cast into the
air theatrically.

The crowd gasped in awe as the loud speaker announced, *'The Magnificent Ronaldo.'* He threw off his cape and gave a courtly bow to his audience, who cheered and clapped with gusto. His hair was slicked back, emphasising his beak nose and in that light his kohl pencilled eyes had a yellow tinge. His black outfit melded into the darkness of the stage behind and he looked truly sinister.

The Mayor, who was standing close by me nodded in my direction saying, 'It's theatre! They call him the paper man you know. He does illusions, tricks with paper.'

'Yes.' I knew his nickname and that in the Spanish Magic circle his illusions were much admired and envied by some.

To my relief, the show went without a hitch in spite of my trepidation. He performed a variety of paper illusions that were enjoyed by both parents and children. Spirits were high and laughter and excited squeals hung around in the atmosphere.

The time passed easily and the grand finale was eagerly awaited when an unexpected gust of wind blew through the crowd and in its wake came a iridescent pink cloud of paper butterflies that floated past the people and on into the street where they sparkled under the halogen lights.

All heads looked up and smiled at the enchanting sight.

The children were so captivated they ran along chasing the small pieces of paper, leaping up in the air trying to capture them. The butterflies danced on and so did the children until the sound of their laughter and joy faded into silence.

Those left behind chatted happily about the wonderful sight and the magician's expertise and waited patiently. Time passed and still there was neither magician nor children to be seen but, as the minutes passed, the chatter diminished and disquiet mumbled through the audience.

The villagers looked at the Mayor for answers. He began to visibly shrink under their questioning gaze and then calmed them with a reassuring look and an embracing gesture of hand.

It was more than five minutes but where were the children?

I felt fear and guilt grip me. Where were those children? Should I have warned them about Ronaldo? Would they have listened to me? Would they have blamed me for knowing him? Maybe they would have arrested me as an accomplice.

Once again the loud speaker announced, 'The Magnificent Ronaldo' and, as the bat-like creature reappeared on the stage, there was a uniform intake of breath and the audience stared in anticipation.

Ronaldo walked forward into the light and bowed extravagantly, smiling, then waved forth the excited children who were hiding in the wings. They all rushed forward to their parents holding an offering of an iridescent pink butterfly and hiding churlish grins of deception.

Relieved parents ran forward and hugged their wards whilst joining in the standing ovation of clapping for the magician.

I looked over at Ronaldo and thought there was a glint of recognition in those artful eyes. I nodded to him and he to me. Did he know me from *The Barrio* I wondered?

At that point a noisy green Peugeot drove into the square and out jumped an auburn haired scamp who ran in the direction of the stage calling, 'Papá! Papá!'

An unfamiliar smile widened the magician's face as the boy jumped into his arms and hung onto his neck lovingly.

From behind the car walked a lithe girlish woman with a mass of thick auburn hair. I recognised her instantly and sighed. It was the beautiful Sofia.

My eyes moistened to see the happy family unit and, at that moment a smiling, self-satisfied Mayor put his hand on my shoulder and led me off along the narrow street. *'Vamos'* let's go for a drink.

In the bar, the Mayor greeted the villagers warmly, shook the men's hands, kissed the women's soft cheeks and ruffled the children's hair.

Settled at our table we had more than a few bonding drinks and talked over the evening's event.

'You liked the show?' The Mayor asked me, in a slow measured voice. 'We are lucky that Ronaldo has now come back to Spain. He was in Venezuela you know?'

I just nodded, waiting for the story to unfold.

'Sofia fled and went to stay with my brother's boy, Armando. It seems she *had* to disappear. It was something to do with a family in his Italian hometown. And now she and Ronaldo have young Paco. You`ve seen the boy haven`t you?'

He ordered another drink and my mind raced. Confused, I found it hard to understand what he was telling me…that what I'd always believed to be the truth – indeed, what *everyone* in *The Barrio* believed to be the truth - was a lie. A deception?

The Mayor chatted on…'Young Paco has his mother's eyes and is tall, like his father.' Leaning closer to me his voice lowered to a whisper. 'It seems Ronaldo and Sofia, had to leave Madrid under cover of night - some sort of vendetta against the magician. You know how vicious these families can be when honour is at stake? My brother's boy, Armando, smuggled Sofia out of Spain…'

'To Venezuela?'

'Yes…' The Mayor hesitated.

'And, Ronaldo?'

'Followed later…' His voiced faded into the past and, as I listened, I realised just how clever Ronaldo had been.

We'd all been tricked. Their disappearance had been yet another elaborate, amazing, audacious illusion, cunningly created by *The Magician*!

St Mawes

Tony Carter

Although we lived in Essex in 1942, our house was only about 10 miles as the bomber flies from the London Docks. My sister was a one-year-old baby and I was four and a half. Our young mother was 24 and experiencing a living nightmare. Every night bombs would fall, shrapnel would fly and windows would blast inwards. Sometimes when the warning sounded we made it to the air raid shelter in the garden or under the stairs but frequently there was no time for this.

When Dad came home on leave he immediately rented a cottage for us at St Mawes in Cornwall.

Mum struggled with us, and two large suitcases, to Paddington where we started the long train journey. From Truro it was a taxi to the cottage. There was no electricity and so the elderly lady next door helped us with oil lamps. There was no running water and so we had to struggle to and from the village pump.

Within a few days, Mum had me enrolled at the village school, which was half a mile down the road. After a week or so I was walking there on my own. Unfortunately, I think I was the only outsider and I was bullied. Going to the toilets was the worst because they would piss over me. Sometimes mum would meet me after lessons with my sister in the pram, but usually I was on my own. Like our cottage, the school was on high ground with the

83

land dropping sharply down to the water's edge and the fishing boats.

On the way home one day, I was walking down one of the steep cobbled streets that had flint-faced walls running alongside when I noticed a bicycle on its side, with a woman sitting by it.

I ran down to her and, to this day, I can remember my physical response to what I saw and what I said to her…

'Are you alright?' Is what I remember saying and then her face turned towards me…

Apart from one small patch of white skin on her cheek, everything was one complete mass of post-box red around her eyes, nose, and mouth and, when she tried to say something, she just kept spitting blood.

At the top of the road I noticed a couple walking by. I ran up towards them. 'There's a lady hurt down there,' I cried. They could see her and moved quickly.

I ran to tell the doctor. We had visited him recently and I knew he lived on the far side of the bay. Halfway there, I saw his car coming towards me with a sign 'Doctor' in the windscreen. I waved but he ignored me. I hadn't thought about a telephone.

I went home and told mum but she didn't believe the story. However, enquiries by *The Falmouth Times* soon convinced her with headlines of *Five Year Old Saves Woman's Life*.

The headmaster at school brought me up on the stage and told everyone but, sadly, that didn't stop the bullying.

Apparently the woman was close to dying from blood loss when the doctor reached her. She did make a full recovery and came to see us before we returned to Ilford. On the anniversary of this accident she would send my mother a box of spring daffodils. About fifteen years later, these boxes stopped coming and we assumed she had passed away.

But, at least her end had been delayed.

A Matter of Time

Ed Harvey

I hurry from the Crimewatch studio. I'd appealed directly to the public and made it clear that without fresh evidence the investigation into *The Schoolmaster* killings was heading into a cul-de-sac. I'm anxious to get out of London before the rush hour, but the appeal went beyond agreed parameters and I've been summoned to a meeting with my new boss, Superintendent Bill Kendrick.

As I walk into his office I sense I'm in for a rough ride.

'Last thing I need is a loose cannon,' he says.

'We've found five bodies so far and got nothing to show for it. Thought it was worth a shot, Sir. The public love a vigilante and can't get enough of *The Schoolmaster's* exploits. We're up against it. You never know, someone might come forward.'

'Can you be sure your team will be impartial?'

The question is fair. Public sympathy for the victims has always been muted and, to be honest, most of my team hate conmen as much as pimps and people traffickers: anyone who exploits the weak and vulnerable.

'They know the score,' I say.

Kendrick raises an eyebrow. 'It would seem he has access to classified information. Are we any closer to identifying the source?'

This throws me momentarily, but I recover quickly enough not to give anything away. 'No, not yet.'

'And the latest killing?' Kendrick skims the case notes I'd sent through to him. 'Same MO?'

'On the face of it, yes. A single shot to the head and another calling card, E for Estate Agent, pinned to the victim's shirt.'

'Not much doubt about the motive, then?'

'Revenge, most likely. A property scam in Southern Spain. They'd fleeced dozens of retired couples out of their life savings. Each of the murdered men was involved. The Architect, the Banker, and the Contractor. *The Schoolmaster* hit the headlines long before the Mayor was found with D for Dignitary pinned to his jacket. The media's been on our backs from day one, hoping to second-guess who'll be next.'

'So what's different about the Estate Agent's death?'

'*The Schoolmaster's* always left evidence of his next victim's involvement – without naming him, of course - but this time he didn't. Maybe he's settled the account.'

Kendrick looks across the table, as if trying to intimidate me. 'So, when can I expect an arrest?'

'The noose is tightening. Technology, forensics and hard graft. It's only a matter of time. We're working through a list of those who lost money, matching their DNA to samples we've found at the scene of each killing. We're looking for a British, white male.'

'Well, that narrows it down.'

I ignore his sarcasm and Kendrick purses his lips and glances down at the file. 'The gun used in the killings..?'

'A Glock 17.'

'Standard issue: Specialist Firearms Officers.'

I feel blood coursing up my neck. 'It might be standard issue,' I say, 'but it could have been sourced from any one of a thousand web sites.'

'Just make sure I'm the first to know if any of our SFOs are involved.'

The grilling goes on for another half-an-hour before he begins to shuffle paper, checks his watch and gets ready to leave. I'm dismissed but, as I'm packing my briefcase, Kendrick comes over and stands too close for comfort. 'So, Emma, how are they treating you at Homicide Command?'

'Treating me?'

'It's early days, I know, but get a result - arrest *The Schoolmaster* and make it stick - and you'll be halfway there.'

'What, like earning Brownie points?'

He laughs and places a hand on my shoulder. I tense and he holds his hands up like a ham actor in an old western. 'Anything wrong, Emma?'

'A bit invasive, if you don't mind me saying so, Sir.' I turn to leave.

'How's your mum?' he says.

They'd probably met, way back, at a police function. 'She's found a half-decent bloke. Living in Crickhowell, South Wales. Happier than I've seen her for years.'

'And your father?'

I saw it coming, but it still feels like a knife plunging into my gut. 'No idea. Haven't seen him for twenty years.'

'He was under my command towards the end of his career,' Kendrick says. 'He was a good cop.'

'So everyone keeps telling me, Sir.'

I take the tube to Notting Hill, go home and leave a note for Alex, asking her to call me, knowing she'll be really pissed off because I've had to cancel again.

Traffic on the M4 is light and around dusk I'm within striking distance of the Severn Bridge. As I join the queue at the toll, I glance at the CCTV camera. I'm confident there's nothing odd about this journey, nothing that would seem unusual or questionable…just me, on my way to see my mum in Crickhowell…except I'm not heading for Crickhowell.

I leave the motorway, bypass Cardiff, and drive south towards Barry.

I turn into a single-track, no-through lane, and hesitate at the entrance to Uncle Peter's cottage.

I turn off the engine and hold on to the steering wheel as though I need to steady a world that's spinning faster than usual. A slideshow of images flicker before me: my mother, twenty years ago, her face full of anger and disgust; *The Schoolmaster's* crime scene photographs and mug shots of his victims; the crude, raucous banter of my team in the bar of Sanctuary House after a long day; and Uncle Peter smiling reassuringly.

Uncle Peter isn't my uncle, of course, but for years he was a friend of the family and worked alongside my father in CID and Special Ops.

A year into retirement, he'd called to tell me he'd been diagnosed with terminal cancer. I went down to take him to his first chemo session and, during a long delay at the clinic, he told me what he intended to do with the time he had left...

Six months later *The Schoolmaster* struck for the first time.

I look up and, in the gloom of the failing light, I see Uncle Peter leaning on the five-bar gate. He waves - a small gesture - and eases the gate open.

The cottage is cramped and ramshackle, with a galley kitchen and parlour on the ground floor, and one bedroom and bathroom upstairs. It was, he'd told me, all he could afford on his pension.

'Emma.' He envelops me in his arms. 'It's so good to see you.'

I make no effort to untangle myself. Over the years, his love has always been unconditional and honourable, and he's the only man I've allowed under my defences.

He hugs me once more and leads me into the parlour.

The fire in the inglenook has been lit, chasing away the chill of the evening. One end of the room is cluttered: newspaper cuttings pinned to overhead beams; a makeshift incident board propped against the back of a chair; files scattered on a floor that's covered with a sheet of polythene.

'Someone's been busy,' I say.

'I thought it best to sort things out.' He hesitates. 'Thanks for coming at such short notice.'

'After the Estate Agent, I was expecting your call.'

'Have you seen today's papers?' He rummages through a pile of notebooks and files strewn across the sofa. 'Front-page. Still hitting the headlines.' His eyes are watering and he pushes sparse strands of silver hair from his forehead. 'There's something rather distinguished about a schoolmaster, don't you think?'

'The Met's profiler reckons he's a loner, unemployed, and sexually inadequate,' I say.

He laughs and shakes his head. 'So predictable.'

'Yes, but it's only a matter of time. Once the dots are joined...'

He holds the newspaper against his chest. 'The press are speculating, of course. The next victim…'

'The letter F, for *Friend*.' It's my turn to hesitate. 'You think he knows?'

'Yes, of course. He's not stupid. He'll know the trail leads to his door.' He drops the newspaper on the sofa and goes to the sideboard. 'Something to calm your nerves?'

'Scotch. Thanks. Small one. Very small one.'

We sit in silence for a few minutes and, as the whisky eases the queasiness in my stomach, I hear a car at the top of the lane.

'Show time.' Uncle Peter heads upstairs.

Tyres crunch on the gravel and the car's diesel engine rattles as it comes to rest.

The suspense seems to last for ever before the engine dies and there's silence.

I watch through a small, curtained window.

My father clambers from his SUV and tucks his shirt into the waistband of his ill-fitting jeans.

I haven't seen him since mum and I left home. He looks older than his years. He's stooped. His hair is a shock of white and his paunch spills over his belt.

He hesitates, then walks towards the front door.

For some reason, when the knock comes it startles me.

'It's open,' Uncle Peter calls, pausing halfway down the stairs.

I watch the door open and my father steps into the parlour. He looks down at the floor and around the room. I step away from the window, the light behind me disguising my appearance momentarily.

'You made it then?'

'Jesus Christ, you startled me,' he says. He takes a moment, as though struggling to recognise me. 'Emma? I wasn't expecting…' his voice trails off. 'I don't understand. What the hell are you doing here?'

'I invited her.' As Uncle Peter takes the last of the stairs, his hands in his jacket pockets. He steps across the room and stands beside me. 'A few loose ends, Gareth,' he says. 'Thought you'd like to tell us why?'

'Tell you what?'

'No, Gareth. Tell us *why*?'

'This a joke? A riddle? Am I supposed to know what you're talking about?'

'Didn't expect you to volunteer information, but thought this might help refresh your memory.'

Uncle Peter pulls a handgun from his jacket and begins to attach a silencer.

'Peter?' My father looks confused.

'A Beretta,' Uncle Peter says. 'The Glock will tie me to the other deaths, but not to yours.'

'Peter, for God's sake.'

'F is for Friend.' Uncle Peter's voice is calm, as though he's rehearsed what to say. 'A friend who conned me into parting with my life savings. I poured everything I had, every penny, into their grubby hands. And, you took your cut, didn't you?'

'I lost as much as you. We were both victims.'

'The file,' Uncle Peter says. 'The one at your feet. Pick it up.' He waits whilst my father flips through the loose-leaf pages. 'It's all there. Copies of bank statements, land-registry documents, the deeds naming you as the owner of the house you bought with the proceeds, photographs of you with the syndicate. Proof. Evidence of your involvement. The sort of proof I left with the other bodies – men who were part of your sordid conspiracy: the architect, the banker, the contractor, the dignitary, and the estate agent – A, B, C, D, and E.' Uncle Peter hesitates. 'The newspaper, on the sofa, look at the headline.'

My father picks it up, glances at it, shakes his head and throws it on the floor. 'You must be out of your fucking mind.'

'You're last on my list. I didn't leave your file with the Estate Agent's body because I didn't want to compromise Emma. Your death will be unrelated to my other victims – a random killing, perhaps, or the sort of underworld retaliation we read about…' Uncle Peter pauses and I wonder how long he'll be able to maintain his composure and how long his strength will last. 'That bastard Estate Agent was so silver-tongued…but you dispelled any doubts I might have had and I fell hook, line and sinker. You must have thought me a fool. You certainly took me for one.'

'I don't know what to say. How can I convince you that I was lucky, that's all?' My father steps forward. 'Look, Peter,' he says. 'Please, put the gun down. Let's talk about this.'

'I lost everything,' Uncle Peter says, quietly.

And, I know what he means.

The cost of the scam was far more devastating than the money involved. His wife died within six months and there was no doubt in Uncle Peter's mind what had broken her heart.

My father looks at me. 'Emma?'

'This is long overdue,' I say.

He looks at us and laughs, harshly.

'You're crazy, both of you.'

But his smile fades and I see desperation in his eyes.

'Peter,' he says. 'Put the gun down.' He points at me. 'Normally, I wouldn't give a shit about her, but you've killed five men. She can make it go away, close the case; lack of evidence. You know how it works. It'll be our secret.'

I retch and taste vomit in the back of my throat.

*Our little secret…*The words he'd whispered as he forced himself into me, twenty years ago.

I was twelve years old.

'We can work something out,' he says. 'I've got money. I'll sell up. Turn myself in. Anything you say but, for God's sake, put the gun down.'

Uncle Peter turns to me.

'Have we heard enough?'

'Yes,' I say. 'It's time.'

There's no ceremony.

No final words.

And no reprieve.

Uncle Peter moves me gently to one side, levels the handgun and pulls the trigger.

The bullet takes milliseconds to impact, hitting its target with a suppressed ferocity that forces my father's body to crumple and fall backwards.

In the silence that follows, I walk to where he has fallen. 'A body shot?'

'The head would have been a giveaway.'

I'm searching for signs of life when the shrill of my mobile phone cuts through the air.

It's Alex.

'Hey,' I say. 'No, no I'm fine. Made good time, but had a flat tyre on the Welsh side of the bridge. Yeah, miss you too. I'm thinking of coming home. No, mum didn't know I was on my way, so she'll be none-the-wiser. Yes, yes, OK. Well, maybe we can both come down next weekend. Look, I've got to change this bloody wheel, so it'll take me a few hours to get back. I might decide to catch a bite to eat in a motorway café or go into Cardiff and stop-over for the night. See how I feel. Yes, catch you tomorrow. Bye. Bye, bye.' I cut the call.

'She OK?'

'Alex? Yes, good as gold. So, what now?'

'We roll him up in the polythene and get rid of anything that might incriminate you.'

'I feel another scotch coming on,' I say.

'Not for me.' His face is etched with the drama of the last few minutes. 'I don't want to be stopped driving a car that doesn't belong to me, with a body in the boot, do I?'

I smile. 'The Mendips?'

'Yes. Far enough away and easily accessible.'

'So, this is the end of *The Schoolmaster*?'

'Yes.' Uncle Peter says. 'It's the end.'

We're back. Sitting in the parlour, the fire and a generous slug of scotch warding off the chill.

He doesn't take his eyes off the flames as he tells me the cancer has spread and it's a matter of days.

He cries. We both cry. And I hold him.

The next few weeks are the shortest of my life. Soon after his doctors confirm there is nothing more they can do except keep him comfortable, Uncle Peter makes his last trip into Cardiff where he uses a payphone to call the Crimewatch hotline.

I'm summoned to a meeting with Superintendent Kendrick. 'The caller said he'd seen the appeal on TV,' I tell him. 'Said he wants to turn himself in.'

'And you know him?'

'As a kid. He worked with my father in Special Ops. He kept in touch with my mum over the years. He's been seriously ill. Mum's helped out where she could.'

'And you had no idea?'

'That he's *The Schoolmaster*? Of course not… What the hell's that supposed to mean?'

'I don't like coincidences.'

'I'm not overjoyed about it myself.'

Kendrick sighs, heavily. 'The press are going to have a field day. We need a conviction. Get on to ballistics and the Crime Scene Investigators. Find the gun he used.' He gets up and goes over to the window. I sense he's suspicious, but doesn't have the final pieces of the jigsaw. 'You're arresting him today?'

'I've got a tactical firearms unit on stand-by. We'll go mob-handed just in case he's armed.'

There is no need for armed response, of course, but I can't explain why *The Schoolmaster* doesn't pose a threat and so, under cover of darkness, I accompany three Armed Response Vehicles down the M4 and across the Severn.

Uncle Peter's arrested. He's taken to Belmarsh Prison, but dies before the Crown Prosecution Service has time to put a case together. His death triggers a post-mortem and an IPCC investigation, and the Coroner has to wait until enquires have been completed before turning the body over to his family.

The funeral is low-key.

His son attends, dignified and unwilling to accept his father has killed five men. He's convinced that if the case had gone to trial he would have been exonerated. I don't have the heart to tell him that a Sunday tabloid will be devoting two pages to an exposé.

I sit at the back of the crematorium. Officially I'm representing the Met, but I wasn't expecting Kendrick to be here. 'I'm sorry to hear about your father, Inspector,' he says, sitting next to me, his voice barely above a whisper. 'It must have been quite a shock.'

I stare ahead.

'The body was found by ramblers, near Cheddar Gorge. Any idea what he was doing there?'

'I haven't seen him for twenty years.'

I watch latecomers take their seats.

'Trouble is,' Kendrick says, 'there are so many unanswered questions. Forensics are convinced he died elsewhere. Couldn't find a cartridge, you see. Shot through the heart. The bullet lodged in his spine, but no cartridge.'

'If the media speculation is only half-right,' I say, 'it could have been someone with a grudge, an old score to settle, a pro with the nous to clear up after him.'

'Yes, yes, of course.'

The minister walks over to Uncle Peter's son and expresses his condolences.

'CCTV footage has you on the M48, crossing the Severn minutes after your father's car crossed on the M4.'

'I was on my way to see my mother but had a puncture on the Welsh side of the bridge. Alex, my partner, called. I turned round and drove back...'

He raises an eyebrow and tilts his head slightly.

The minister stands before the congregation and the opening bars of *Land of My Fathers* blares from the sound system.

'CSIs found the Glock in a cupboard under the stairs. Your Uncle Peter didn't go to too much trouble trying to hide it.'

'Good,' I say. 'I hate loose ends.'

'You know...' Kendrick leans across, his face too close for comfort. 'I've found it strangely compulsive, this soap opera that's played out before us. Your father, your Uncle Peter, and you...' He pauses and I sense he's enjoying my discomfort. 'You understand why I found it so intriguing?'

'Look, if you have any doubts...'

'Doubts? No, I don't have any doubts, none at all. Not since my chat with Alex.'

'Excuse me?'

'That's why I'm late. I knew you'd be tied up down here. We picked her up this morning, had a couple of questions for her.'

I flinch and telltale blotches flood my neck. The music reaches its climax as male voices swell into the rafters.

'She was very cooperative,' I hear Kendrick say. 'Eager to provide that all important alibi.'

'I need an alibi?'

'Where you were on the night your father was murdered. What time you got home.'

'You could have asked me.'

'Best to be certain when it's one of our own, don't you agree?' He smiles and I want to smack his face.

The minister invites everyone to join in prayers. We stand in silence for a several moments.

'Crimewatch called,' Kendrick whispers. 'They want you on their next show.'

'The officer who arrested *The Schoolmaster* is the daughter of a murdered cop?'

'Makes for good TV, apparently.'

'Yes, but it's not going to happen. I wasn't cut out for show business and besides I've got enough on my plate.'

'*The Schoolmaster's* a good result. Something that'll look good on your CV.' Kendrick pauses…'I just can't help wondering if he would have turned himself in *without* your involvement.'

I lift my head and drag air into my lungs as the coffin slips silently from view.

I can't help, but smile. 'Your guess is as good as mine, Sir.' I look at him. 'But, we'll never really know for sure, will we?'

The Flood

Jean McGrane

Tyrannic river, wielding boulders,
scoured past my door:
Bleating cars and ram rod tree trunks
tossed within its maw.
Deadly flume choking homes
with sewer reeking mud.
Walls torn open; a kitchen bared
– made naked by the flood.

The pathetic flapping of a yellow checked curtain,
Supper dishes in the sink.

As torrent stalled, the flying ants
obeyed a call to swarm;
Crept from deep within the soil
– wings folded, maggoty form.
Black rippling magma
they flowed unheeding,
Their passage to life
over gorged rivers' leavings.

The reeds; plastic bottles and bloated bruised hand –
Its ragged mud filled nails.

Barely a Holiday

Ian Patrick

Bert and Olive live in a terraced street in Leeds. Bert worked as overseer in a shirt factory for forty years and Olive was a seamstress in an underwear factory. They were both made redundant when their respective factories were unable to compete with imported goods from the Far East.

They have no children and have not had a proper holiday since they were married over thirty years ago (taking Bert's pigeons to Scotland for the annual fanciers' convention was not Olive's idea of a holiday!) Now, with their redundancy money sitting proudly in their bank account, a proper holiday is on the cards.

Scene 1

Bert and Olive are sitting in front of the coal fire in their living room. There are two armchairs with large leather arms pulled up to the fire. Behind the armchairs is an unvarnished kitchen table next to the window and next to the table a large sideboard takes pride of place. On the floor a clip rug covers the linoleum.

Olive is wearing a headscarf over her curlers and a pinny covers her skirt. Her stockings have holes in them and she has an old pair of slippers more or less on her feet.

Bert is wearing a shirt without a collar and trousers held up by braces. On his head he wears the flat cap that is only removed when he goes to bed and he has nothing on his feet except his socks.

Olive

I'm sick to death of this damned weather. Every day the same, grey skies and if it's not raining, it's freezing cold.

Bert

Cheer up lass. It's not long before we'll be going on holiday. You're looking forward to going away, aren't you?

Olive
No, I'm damn well not.

Bert
(Shocked)
You're not. Why?

Olive

Now just you listen to me Bert, I do not intend to spend these summer holidays taking those perishing pigeons to Scotland and having to listen to you and the rest of your cronies cooing with the birds.

Bert

But love, we always take the pigeons to Scotland. If we don't go they'll get broody.

Olive

Broody is it? Well I'll tell you here and now, if you mention Scotland again, you'll be having pigeon pie for your dinner.

Bert winces in alarm.

Bert

Where do you want to go, then?

Olive

Somewhere that's hot and sunny. Now get yourself out and bring some brochures back with you.

Bert pulls on his shoes and leaves the room muttering to himself.

Scene 2

Bert returns with an armful of brochures.

Olive

You took your time – I thought you'd gone on holiday by yourself.

Bert
(Aside)
I wish

Olive
What was that?

Bert

Nothing love. Here's the brochures. Have a look and see what you think.

Olive scans the brochures and throws them at Bert in disgust.

Olive

Scarborough, Whitby, Skegness and Cromer are not what I'd call hot and don't you dare suggest Blackpool.

Bert

Well according to Charlie, it may be a bit hotter in Sellafield, Hartlepool, Sizewell or Dungeness.

Olive

That's because they're nuclear power stations, you muppet. Anyway where did you meet Charlie?

Bert
In the 'Dog and Duck'.

Olive

So that's where you were all this time. I might have known. Now you can get yourself off again and this time get me a proper holiday. Somewhere I can get a nice suntan.

Bert puts on his coat and goes out again.

Scene 3

Bert comes into the living room staggering as he does so. He has obviously paid another visit to the 'Dog and Duck'. He shouts for his wife to come into the room.

Bert
Olive! Olive dearest, I've got something to tell you.

Olive comes into the room, scowling as she wipes her hands on a tea towel.

Olive
What is it? What do you want?

Bert
I've got a surprise for you. I've booked a holiday.

Olive
(Incredulously)
You've done what?

Bert
Booked a holiday.

Olive
Where?

Bert
(Triumphantly)
Spain.

Olive
(In amazement)
What on earth possessed you to choose Spain? It's full of Spaniards and we can't speak Spanish.

Bert
We don't have to speak Spanish. There's lots of English who live over there and they don't speak the language either, so Charlie said.

Olive
Oh, you've been with him again. I might have known. Anyhow, whereabouts in Spain are we going?

Bert
It's a place called Vera, near Mo-ja-car. *(Said as spelt)*

Olive
I've heard of Redcar, but I've never heard of Mo-ja-car. Is it near Benidorm? Our Ethel went there once and she said that it was full of lager louts.

Bert
No, Vera and Mo-ja-car are a long way from there. Charlie told me that they were nice quiet places.

Olive
How long are we going for?

Bert

Two weeks. Charlie said that he'd look after my pigeons but I expect that they'll still pine for me. We'll have to get passports you know.

Olive

What – for the pigeons?

Bert

No. For us of course.

Olive

You haven't said exactly when we're going.

Bert

The week after next.

Olive

You haven't given me much warning. I'll have to get some new clothes and a swimming costume.

Bert

Why don't you wait and get them in Spain? They'll have all the latest fashions over there.

Olive

I suppose you're right – mind you this place had better be good Bert, or you'll be for it.

Olive goes back out of the room   whilst Bert pokes the fire and settles in the armchair.

Scene 4

Bert and Olive have arrived in Spain. It was dark when they reached their apartment and being tired after their journey, they went straight to bed. Now, at eight thirty in the morning, having washed and dressed, they come into the lounge. Olive is wearing a summer blouse and skirt and her hair has been styled. Bert still wears his collarless shirt and trousers held up with braces. He has bought some new sandals, which he wears over calf length socks. Olive opens the blinds.

Olive

Oh Bert, look at that lovely sunshine. Isn't it hot here? In fact it's so hot that I had to take off my nightie in the middle of the night.

She looks at Bert suggestively.

Bert
Did you? – I didn't notice.

Olive
Oh Bert, I'm so excited. Let's go and have a look around before breakfast.

Bert
We'll go on to the balcony – you can get a good view from there.

They go onto the balcony and revel in the sight of the large swimming pool underneath their balcony and the long sandy beach in front of a sea so blue that it takes their breath away.

Olive
(Putting her head on Bert's shoulder)
Bert, this is paradise. Thank you so much.

Before Bert can reply, they see a couple walking towards the pool. Then from another direction two men appear. Bert rubs his eyes in disbelief.

Olive
Bert, Bert!! No-one's got any clothes on. They are all stark naked.
Bert, what is this place?

Bert
(Dumbfounded)
Well Charlie recommended it. He said that you'd get a good suntan here.

Olive
Let me look at that brochure.
(She looks at the brochure)
Oh Bert, you've booked us into a nudist colony.
What are we going to do now?

Bert
(Takes down his braces and removes his shirt).
We might as well join them. Come on lass don't be shy. You did say you wanted a good suntan.

Olive
(Taking off her skirt)
I didn't mean all over, you clown. I'll swing for that bloody Charlie.

And that is how Bert and Olive became naturists.

You Can Run

Beth Goldsworthy

Jean Luc ducked, narrowly avoiding the flying saucer. It hit the wall and exploded, spraying shrapnel for meters. He raced for the door and didn't stop to think until he was driving down the road, away from his house and his crazy wife - his hell on earth.

A quick glance in his rear-view mirror showed Gracie standing at the end of the drive watching him speed away. Fuck it. He loved her, but the price was much too high. The stress was overwhelming and he wanted to get as far as possible away from her and the living hell he had endured for far too long. He had the battle scars to prove it and couldn't trust that the next one might not be fatal.

The last time he'd left, she'd tracked him down, ruthlessly, and begged and bargained for a rematch. He'd given in and gone quietly, hoping she would keep her promises: no more violence; no more tantrums, childish jealousies or hysterics.

That had lasted, what, six weeks? Maybe less. Then Jill, his PA from work, phoned him at home to give him an urgent message that needed his instant attention and Gracie went into one of her dangerously quiet sulks. He knew how that would play out. First off, she would try to make sense of how she was feeling. Then, she'd invent her own truth about Jill and fall off the edge and lose it big time. She'd start by screaming at him - blaming him for not loving her enough, for needing other women - and then accuse him of a range of misdemeanours that were really in her head and not a reality at all.

What Jean Luc needed most of all was a quiet sanctuary, a place to feel safe and peaceful. He needed time to take stock of his life and decide where he was going.

With Gracie, his life had been one long trauma. He knew in his heart that he loved her, but could not continue living with her insecurities, jealousies, tantrums and, most of all, her violence.

He had suggested to her that, maybe, she should seek help: see someone, a doctor or even a shrink. But there'd been no 'maybe' about it. She'd gone ballistic, throwing things and screaming and finally crying and begging him to forgive her.

Over the years, he'd found it harder to love her, harder to get anywhere near her...

He drove to work and, as he walked into his office, a hush fell over the room.

'Fuck,' he thought, 'I've missed the meeting.' He threw his briefcase down next to his desk.

Jill knew about some of the problems he'd had at home. She gave a little cough. 'Mark wants to see you, immediately, if not sooner,' she said, and he sensed regret in her voice.

'I've screwed up this time, haven't I?'

She smiled, thinly.

As he headed for the 'snake pit', he felt he was sinking in a sea of treacle and his chest was tight and his stomach had knotted.

Mark was not happy. He looked up from his desk and his eyebrows lifted in a way that made him look like a viper about to strike - hence 'the snake pit'.

'You look like shit,' Mark said. 'What the hell's going on? You missed the meeting. I can't let this go. You know that, don't you?'

Jean Luc did not reply.

'And don't give that bullshit about your crazy wife…'

'I've left her,' Jean Luc muttered.

'What?'

'I've left her.'

'Seriously?' Mark sat down.

'I can't carry on like this. This time it's for real. I want my life back.' Jean Luc sank into an armchair and held his head in his hands.

Silence.

Mark poured him a coffee. 'Look, if you really mean that, I have an idea.'

Jean Luc looked up. Was Mark throwing him a lifeline?

'We're opening a branch in Singapore. I need a good man over there. With your linguistic talents, I think you could be the right person for the job. There'll be a six-month trial. You'll be on probation, but any hint of personal problems getting in the way of work, then that'll be it. Just get it sorted. You understand?'

'I'll divorce her. Start again. It's just going to take some time. Gracie will fight me all the way.'

'Best get yourself a good lawyer.'

Jean Luc made an appointment to see Paul Creasey, a well-known divorce lawyer and a good friend. 'I'm going to Singapore and I don't want her to know where I am. The last time I tried to end our relationship was scary enough, and I don't want to go through that again. She scares the shit out of me and I need to get as far as possible from her.'

'She can't put a stop to proceedings, once they're under way,' Paul explained. 'And you don't need to be here.'

Jean Luc thought he detected a hint of sadness in Paul's voice. He'd known them both at University, of course. They'd been his friends, separately, and he'd introduced them - something he probably regretted, now. Gracie had fallen in love with Jean Luc - hook, line and sinker - but her love became obsessive and, over the years, Paul would have seen her change from a carefree young student into a demented she-wolf.

Paul was best man at their wedding and had helped them buy their first home. Now he was orchestrating their divorce.

Jean Luc was sitting in an elegant bar. He looked at the twinkling lights of the city and across the Singapore Straits glistening under a moonlit sky, towards the outlying islands.

God, this felt good.

He loved his new life.

His new flat was modern, clean, neat and functional. There were no cushions. No lined, expensive fabrics to soften it. Just lots of light and, although it was only about 50m2, it felt like 5000.

115

He had his personal space.

And business was going well.

Jean Luc was a natural diplomat and that made dealing in Singapore a lot easier. His command of French - his mother tongue - helped. There were a surprising number of French speaking Chinese and they loved it when he spoke French to them. And, with his flair for languages, his Mandarin was coming on in leaps and bounds. He was the ideal appointment and back in England, Mark was more than happy with the results.

He took another sip of his Singapore sling and thought just how perfect life was. He selected a savoury snack that had been served with his drink and marvelled at its taste and delicate nature.

That was something else new; different.

He finished his cocktail and ordered a whisky. It was good to try different things, he thought, but nothing could beat a real drink.

He watched the barmaid pour his Scotch. She had a confidence and flair. Maybe, after she'd finished work…

He smiled.

He felt good.

He felt safe.

He lifted his head and adjusted his tie.

He glanced in the mirror that lined the back of the bar and froze.

'Hello, darling.'

Howl

MarianMay Simpson

A dark shape appeared on the ridge, silhouetted against the dusky evening sky, forming a part of the undulating mountain outline. The horned Ibex came to the same spot most evenings, keeping vigil in his high position, watching and listening to the sounds coming from the valley below. His valley.

Various noises drifted upwards from the village, soft flamenco music played on an old guitar, a barking dog or the sound of a football being patted around the pitch.

He knew these human sounds well but they meant nothing to him. He was on the alert for predators that lay in wait for nightfall, ready to attack defenceless animals as they scuttled about. He was poised and ready to move as quickly as he could down the mountainside, ready to lock horns with the enemy in defence of his valley of creatures.

This evening seemed different, he could sense something in the cold, evening air, so he waited and watched.

Suddenly, the quiet was broken by a single howl, followed by a chorus of barking and squealing. The noisy fracas reached screaming pitch and then suddenly stopped.

It was over in seconds, followed by a deathly silence, except for the soft winds floating downwards, whispering, sending out the news.

Hours passed. The sky darkened as night fell on the valley. The village lamps came on, casting ghostly, tree shaped shadows on the empty streets.

He waited and listened. There was only silence. The gypsy guitarist had stopped playing his music and the merry footballers had gone home.

From miles away came the buzzing swarm, as if answering a call, filling the valley with an unwelcome sound, their presence closing in, confirming the passing of a friend.

The horned silhouette heard the drone and knowing there was nothing to be done, he hung his head, slowly climbed over the mountain ridge and disappeared.

City Kids

Linda Burton-Cooper

Leon brushed his waxed hair back with the heel of his hand creating the much-desired designer look worn by most of the boys on his block.

Heading for the front door he slipped his mobile and door keys deep into his pocket, and then sneaked a quick glance in the mirror. With a tilt of the head, he gave himself a nod of approval. Leon was a good-looking boy and he knew it.

'Take a fiver outta me purse and wrap up son, its cold out there. And take that jacket Errol left behind as well.'

'Will do mum,' he shouted back. He took the neatly folded five pound note from her purse leaving only a few remaining coins that would have to get them through the rest of week end.

His mother, in her early thirties, was a plump pale-faced woman with straggly blonde hair who spent most of her time curled up on the settee watching television and eating snack bars. Leon was her only child. His dad had left when Leon was a baby and now, at sixteen, he saw himself as the man of the house. He felt a deep need to protect his loving but as he thought, clueless mother.

That was more than he could say for his dad who, it would seem, preferred life in Nigeria to that of living on the 5th floor of a block of council flats in South East London caring for his girlfriend and growing son.

He had seen pictures of his dad and looked like him - tall, slim and handsome. Leon's skin was more of a coffee colour and he had his mum's hazel eyes.

'Bye,' he called out and with the jacket draped over his shoulder, swaggered out of the flat and headed for the lift.

When he saw the *Out of Order* notice sellotaped to the door, he cursed angrily and threw a snap kick at it leaving a stencilled trainer print as a mark of outrage knowing, as did the other residents especially the elderly living on the top levels, that it would not be repaired until after Monday, sometime!

Boyishly, he ran down the stairs sliding along the banisters, weightless, free, and thrilled with excitement. Reaching the ground floor feeling exhilarated he swung open the exit door and walked out into the estate square.

Seeing the streetlights and hearing familiar voices he put away childish things, donned a cool swagger walk and mingled amongst his peers.

After the ritual shoulder slapping and bonding handshakes, he proudly told his mates, 'I'm off to do me community service man.' And then headed off to the nearby bus stop.

Away from the shelter of the high rise flats it was much colder but he would rather have frozen than wear that jacket of Errol's, it was naff, but his mum had insisted that he took it, so he did.

Pulling up his sweatshirt hood to ward off the chill he became just another anonymous black hooded figure moving like a shadow in the early evening winter dark.

The jacket slung over his shoulder had been discarded, along with a quarter bottle of whisky, by Errol, one of his so-called uncles who, bleary-eyed one morning, had kissed his mum goodbye, never to be seen again.

'Probably went off to Nigeria to join me dad,' he scoffed, but Leon felt a hollowness in his chest that threatened to bring tears to his eyes.

Pulling himself upright his inner voice came pushing through, *'Leon you're a man, not a child, you've gotta be 'ard man. It's an 'ard world boy. Ya gotta guard yarself,'* he worded in his local gang patois.

As he repeated the familiar mantra he could feel a metaphysical armour built up around his chest and grip his heart.

He sauntered off and leaping onto the first passing bus was speedily transported to Leicester square tube station where his mate Ben was waiting. The boys greeted each other with their usual ritual of hugging and high fiving and then waited not so patiently for their probation officer to arrive. They had met one another through Miss Wigget and had named her affectionately Miss Twiglet. 'She's thin, brown and snappy, she looks like a Twiglet man,' Ben had said cheekily. And so the nickname had stuck, but they both liked and respected her and her jaunty manner.

This evening was her community service idea, something they would not have thought about let alone have chosen to do.

121

Ben swung from a lamppost out into the road and searched the stream of pedestrians marching along the pavement hoping to catch a glimpse of her.

'Where is she?' he grumbled restlessly.

Leon liked Ben and when he was in his company he felt like they were brothers. They had a lot in common. Both had a history of shoplifting, particularly stealing designer trainers and now they shared the same probation officer.

Leon remembered sadly the first time his mother had collected him from the police station, he was only thirteen and she was crying. Now at sixteen he was a fully-fledged juvenile delinquent. 'What do they expect of us man, no money, no work?' Leon spat out at an unsuspecting passer by who looked bemused. He kicked the lamp post in frustration.

'What time is it?' Ben grumbled. 'Where is she man? Hey! Here she comes.' They watched as Miss Wigget made her way towards them in a long woollen coat, boots and a knitted hat.

'What a sight,' Ben said, his tone mocking and sarcastic. Ben had a way with words and that was one of the things Leon most admired about him. 'Look at her, Leon. We're not catching the Northern Line to *The Arctic* are we?

'Miss Wigget bounded up to them with a big smile and said, 'Evening boys.'

'Hello Miss Wigget,' they chorused back.

In her usual pragmatic way she marched them off into the hordes of Christmas shoppers, snaking her way adeptly through the driven, baggage-laden people.

The two boys easily skipped, dodged and dived through the relentless crowds, closely behind her.

Suddenly she stopped, did an eyes right and waved the boys in the direction of a narrow Soho street.

The three of them walked shoulder to shoulder down the mews toward the *Food Share* van where the queue of homeless people waited patiently.

The boys were introduced to the organiser, a kindly avuncular man wearing a retro duffle coat and woollen hat whose eyes danced with enthusiasm as he deployed the volunteers and reassured the queue that the food would be served up soon.

Ben and Leon were placed behind the serving trays - ladles and spoons at the ready. They started feeding the hungry souls who, Leon guessed, were not there out of choice but out of desperation. The boys sensed there was a feeling of grab and run in the air.

Leon, smelling and seeing the delicious food recently donated by local supermarket chains, was overwhelmed with hunger. Compared with the two spam sandwiches his mother had served up for his tea this meal would be a banquet.

His own needs took a back seat as the downtrodden hungry people offered up their plates for a serving.

Very few looked at him, they just shoved their plates forward in a complacent manner eager to take whatever was given with unspoken expectation.

It was obvious to Leon that the survival instinct was stronger for some than for others. The more determined waddled off in layers of clothing, fabric and newspaper to ward off the chilling cold of the pavements at night. The others, less hardy, were scantily clad by comparison and somewhat prey to the cold hard city.

After all the food was eaten, the volunteers cleaned up and packed away everything so efficiently that no one would have known that anyone had been there let alone some sixty people fed.

As the vagrants started to disperse - setting off in search of a comfortable pitch - Leon boldly went amongst them wishing them all a Merry Christmas.

Most shuffled away disinterested. They had had what they had come for and were eager to find somewhere to settle for the night after having been warmed by a stomach full of food.

Leon patted the arm of a lean gaunt man who looked cold and worn. 'Merry Christmas, mate.'

The man placed his hand over Leon's and lifting his head said, 'Thanks boy.'

Their eyes met for a flash of a second, the potency in that blink of an eyelid, in that familiar space when two souls meet and they know they are one and the same.

Leon shifted his eyes, overwhelmed by the power of that moment, and then, looking back into the man's face, his heart went out to this man who was near frozen, his thin nose pinched and red, the shadows around his sunken eyes matching the darkness of his hollow cheeks.

Leon took off his tracksuit top and offered it to the man in whose eyes he noticed both pride and resignation. He was glad the man accepted the gift knowing that the winter would get even colder in January.

The man zipped up the top and covered his freezing ears with the hood, sinking his nose into its warmth breathing in he embraced himself as though inhaling the scent of youth and promise.

Leon thought he saw a glint of hope enter the man's dull eyes. Perhaps he might make it through the winter.

'Hey, Leon.' Ben's voice called from the distance. 'Our bus is coming, man.'

Leon skipped away like a child, only stopping to turn and wave goodbye to Miss Wigget and the man, who raised a lean cold hand and smiled.

Back on the block, Leon put on the naff jacket and turned its collar up to keep the outside cold at bay. But, in his heart there was a warm glow.

He knew he was somehow different.

Something inside him had changed.

A small window to his heart had been opened.

Water

Glenis Meeks

I stand at the edge of the pool
like a sentinel, but I cannot drink.
Above, the relentless sun beats down
drying the very sap in my veins.
There is no escape, no shade
to avoid the searing, burning rays.
I am parched, dehydrated, desiccated,
literally dying from thirst.

The rectangular body of pellucid water
alongside me, hard, like sheet glass,
vaporises, evaporates in invisible action,
revealed only by shrinkage to
a lower level of tile.
I feel constricted in my narrow corset
of terracotta pot.
Nowhere to stretch, seek, search.
My very foundations crumble about me,
tantalised, tormented by
the blue, aqueous mass.

A gentle stir of air materialises
causing a tremor on the water.
Molecules split at the surface
as the wind increases speed.
In the hot, blistering gusts, water churns,
splattering pool's edge but not reaching me.

I bend, sway, flow this way, that
in a manic dance, as the Sirocco wind
violently bullies its way across the terrain.
The buffeting is unbearable.
Already weak, I begin to wither, shrivel,
bowed down by the merciless battering
blowing from the scorched Sahara.
Sky darkens.
Was that a raindrop on my head?
Another falls and another…
Pitter, patter, pitter, patter.
I gulp with relief as the restoring water
flows into every nook and crevice.

Vigour, vitality, vivacity,
zip through my veins. I am alive!
I look at the pool, pelted by precipitation,
opaque now, under its barrage.
The Sirocco whirls away
leaving a deposit of sand everywhere
wetted by the pounding rain,
which shows no sign of abating.

Nightfall brings little respite.
The deluge has refilled the pool.
It seethes beside me.
Brimful, murky inky, pluvial.
My pot is engorged, overfull, waterlogged.
Roots sodden, saturated, soggy.
I wilt through excess
and literally drown in despair.

A Most Peculiar Man

Ed Harvey

Inspired by Paul Simon's song
A Most Peculiar Man

I tried to remain positive, but it was difficult. Everywhere I looked along the High Street, there were more shops boarded up than open, more graffiti than invitations to buy, and more rubbish in gutters and doorways than goods on display. There were remnants of past prosperity - cafés promising gut-busting fry-ups; kebab joints catering for the dwindling Turkish community; a general-store selling everything from alcohol to lottery tickets; a launderette, a taxi cab outlet, and two tatty pubs vying for punters craving football on Sky TV. But these oddments weren't enough to convince me that this would be a fascinating, stimulating place to live, where I'd engage in the daily struggle to survive with *real* people.

Still, my priority was to find Flat 37A and at least I was on the right side of the road, where the odd numbered Victorian properties - flats above shops and lists of names under doorbells - had been sub-divided by landlords to maximise profit.

From the recess of a doorway, the stench of cats' urine mingled with the remains of a discarded takeaway and I shuddered.

So, *this* was bedsit land?

Ridiculously, my pulse quickened as I stood outside number 37. It *was* number 37 I needed wasn't it? I looked at the crumpled advert I'd cut from the *Evening Standard* and felt oddly insecure.

A narrow doorway beckoned.

This was to be home.

Home for the foreseeable future.

My home.

As I stood there, the shutter over No 37's shopfront clattered into life, clanked upwards into the recess of twin lintels and disappeared from view. A tall, gangling young man with white jacket over white apron smeared with blood, came out, nodded in my direction, secured the shutter and sauntered back inside. Displayed in the shop window was a vegetarian's nightmare - butchered meat – and selected cuts from each animal had been shoehorned into plastic trays and allocated their own area of the silicon shelf.

The whiff of slaughter drifted towards me and it was at that moment that I first noticed the flies.

Inside the shop, two men were busy preparing for the day whilst a woman, with hair hidden under a white cap, shooed flies away with a flexible swat.

The flies could ruin a butcher's reputation and do more damage to profits than the economic downturn. No one would buy *quality meats at discount prices* when flies were openly gorging themselves.

I was about to enquire after flat number 37A, when the narrow doorway next to the shop opened and an elderly woman looked at me and cracked a toothless smile. Like a poorly rehearsed drag act, she folded ample arms over a floral apron tied tightly around her waist and then adjusted the gaggle of curlers in her thinning white hair.

'You number 37A, *ducks*?' she asked.

I hadn't heard the word *ducks* since my gran passed away. Gran would use *ducks* whenever she couldn't remember someone's name and, whenever I came to stay, she'd call *me* ducks. '*Sit over there, ducks, and take the weight off your feet. Tea, ducks?*' And so it went on. I was never really sure if she knew who I was.

'I've been watching you since you came out of the Tube, lugging that big case about. Ain't it got none of them wheels?' She turned and made her way along the corridor towards a narrow staircase that led, I presumed, to the flats above the butcher's.

'I've been to your room,' she called over her shoulder, 'and put the kettle on. You'd like a cuppa, *ducks*?'

'Yes. Thank you.'

I followed her, my case in my left hand, my right hand brushing away a couple of flies.

'The weather's been very hot and sticky over the last week. Them flies are everywhere. I'll go down the road later and get some spray.'

At the top of the stairs, we turned onto a small landing and stood outside flat 37A.

'Here we are, ducks,' she said. She pulled a key from the pocket of her apron and let herself in. 'It ain't much, but there's a kitchen and a bathroom on the next floor. The electric meter's behind the front door. Takes fifty-pence pieces, same as the water heater in the bathroom. I live upstairs. Number 37C.

I got a lovely view across the roof tops, all the way to the city proper.'

'And 37B?' I asked, assuming there'd be another flat above me.

'Don't ask,' she muttered, shaking her head. 'Funny bloke, if you know what I mean…'

'No, I…'

'Peculiar, I'd say. Keeps 'imself to 'imself. Don't say nothin' to no-one.' She made her way over to a kettle and emptied boiling water into two mugs. 'Mind you, he's the lucky one…'

'Lucky?'

'He's got a kitchenette in his room. With a gas oven, would you believe?' She paused as if wanting to underline the significance of this. 'At least he keeps the bath clean. You mind you clean your scum off when you're done. I don't want no scum left for me to 'ave to scrub before I 'as a soak.'

'I'll do my best.' I smiled and looked around the room. It was large enough, I supposed, for a bed-sit, and spanned the length of the double fronted butcher's shop. Each wall was patterned with dull, lifeless wallpaper of fading green flowers on a beige background. A single bed had been pushed against the wall to my right and a solid-looking chest of drawers was crammed into the corner at the foot of the bed. It reminded me of the shabby rooms in *Rising Damp*, the classic comedy that was enjoying something of a revival on daytime TV.

At the far end of the room, glass doors set into rusting metal frames opened out onto a balcony, its railings just visible through the grime.

'You can open them doors,' she said. 'Outside, there ain't enough room to swing a cat, but you can watch the traffic go by as you sip your morning cuppa.' She paused, handing me one of two mugs of tea. 'You got work to go to?'

I hesitated, wondering how much more of my personal business she'd want to know before she was satisfied and left. She was what my gran would have called a *nosy cow.*

'I'm *between* jobs,' I muttered, and took a sip of tea.

'Unemployed, eh?' She shook her head. 'Lot of it about, ducks. It's them bankers. Stole all that money. Bloody criminal if you ask me.'

'I'm sorry,' I said. 'I don't know your name.'

'Mrs Reardon. Mrs Gladys Reardon.'

'And you're my landlady?'

'Gawd luv us, no, ducks. You gives your rent to the butcher every Saturday morning, in cash.'

'So, he's our landlord?'

She shrugged. 'Search me.'

'And the other tenant?' I asked. 'Is he at home?'

'No idea. Like I says, he don't go out of his way to be sociable. Probably don't give a monkey's for anyone 'cept himself.'

'Peculiar, you said,' I reminded her.

'I don't know, do I? He's odd, that's all. I tried to make him feel at home, but he just ignored me. I ain't never really spoke to 'im since. Most peculiar if you ask me. Never has any visitors, except his brother. He came 'ere once, about a week ago. Last Saturday, I think.'

'His brother?'

'Think that's who 'e was.'

'And no one else, before or since?'

Her eyes narrowed.

''Er, what's wiv all the questions?'

'Just trying to break the ice.' I hesitated. 'Perhaps I ought to go and introduce myself.'

'I shouldn't bother, ducks. He ain't worth it.'

I looked down at my tea and discovered two flies had got there before me. I gave up and, as I put the mug down, I heard the thud of cleaver meeting bone.

'You'll get used to them chopping up that meat and sawing through them bones,' she said. 'You'll get used to the smell after a while, too.' She paused as she took a swipe at several flies circling in the centre of the room.

I walked over to my front door and opened it. 'Thank you, Mrs Reardon,' I said firmly, hoping she'd take the hint. 'It was very kind of you to welcome me and make me feel so at home.'

'Anything you want, ducks. Just pop up. My room's on top floor, above the kitchen.' She was halfway through the door when she turned and added, 'I'll fix my hair and go down the Co-op and get some fly spray. You'll let me have a couple a quid? Help out, like?'

'Half and half,' I said. 'Goodbye, Mrs Reardon.'

Alone in my room, I checked through the drawers of the sideboard. They were lined with aging newspaper but otherwise empty. I looked inside a tall, thin cupboard that housed a tatty dustpan and broom. I scanned the skirting for electric sockets, a telephone plug and TV aerial inlet, and found three sockets, and one aerial, but no telephone.

I'd have to learn to be grateful for small mercies, I supposed. I could no longer afford my mobile, not even pay-as-you-go, and hadn't noticed a payphone as I'd followed Mrs Reardon up the stairs. Maybe there'd be one on the landing outside the bathroom or in the shop? Otherwise it would be a walk to the Tube each time I needed to make a call.

I sat on the bed, sank my chin into my hands, and decided it was no good feeling sorry for myself. I needed a plan. I'd sweep and dust my room, and then call my sister and arrange for her to bring over my stuff. I snorted and shook my head. My *stuff*. A couple of cardboard boxes…

I wasn't sure if I wanted her to come here. She'd only cry and try to persuade me to take the spare room she'd offered when I was evicted after being made redundant.

'It's the downturn,' the boss had said. I knew it was coming, but it was still a shock. I fell behind with payments on the one bedroom flat I'd bought five years ago, went into negative equity and the bank foreclosed.

Mrs Reardon was right; it's bloody criminal what happened.

I'd lost my job, but I'd get another one, wouldn't I?

I sat up, looked around the room, and brushed away several curious flies that had settled on me.

I needed the bathroom and resolved to explore the landing above and introduce myself to the other tenant. He might welcome a fresh face - one that didn't glare disapprovingly at him from beneath a set of curlers.

Mrs Reardon had left a key and I locked my door then climbed the dozen or more stairs.

There was a strong stench that I couldn't place and I assumed it was clogged drains or raw sewage. Leading off the landing were several doors. One was closed and part glazed. The bathroom, I supposed. A second door was ajar and I eased it open to find a kitchen that cried out to be updated.

The sink was ceramic and had several large cracks in it. I lent over and tried to locate the stench. The plughole reeked but had its own distinctive musty smell that a dose of disinfectant would probably shift. I made a mental note to add it to the list of things to buy at the convenience store.

The oven and hob were electric and attached to another meter. It looked as though I'd be cooking pay-as-you-go meals. There was no microwave, so it would be boil-in-the-bag on high-days and holidays. I smiled ruefully when I noticed that there wasn't a washing machine. So, trips to the launderette were set to become part of my routine.

A tall swing-bin in the far corner was crammed with leftovers and discarded packaging. Flies were flitting in and out, their buzzing amplified by the close confines of the bin. Here might be the source of the stench I thought but, although it was disgusting, the smell emanating from the bin was nothing like as strong as the one I'd noticed.

I shuddered, closed the kitchen door, retreated to the bathroom, locked the door, sat on the loo and, in a moment of peace and solitude, I looked out of a half-open sash window at the unkempt garden below.

Moments later, there was a rap on the door and Mrs Reardon's shrill voice clattered through the glass.

'You gonna be long, ducks? Only I gotta go.'

I washed my hands, looked at the sad excuse for a towel draped over the side of the bath and dried them on my jeans before letting her in.

'Thanks, ducks. Can't hold it like I used to.' She closed and locked the door behind her.

I decided to knock on number 37B and walked across the landing towards the door.

The stench intensified.

It was accompanied by a growing discord of flies that seemed to be in swarm and were cramming through a gap at the bottom of the door.

I knocked.

The buzzing amplified.

I knew, instinctively, what lay behind the door. I'd seen enough cop drama on TV and read enough chilling scene-of-crime novels to know. Of course, fiction can only hint at the power of the stench, how overpowering it is, how distinctive, how...God awful. But fiction cannot begin to describe what I felt, *how* I felt, how unable to stop the nausea from rising from my gut, how close I was to hysteria, knowing...

I had every intention of pushing open the door, but the courage to do so deserted me and I turned and hurried down to the butchers' shop.

'A phone!' I demanded. 'Where's your phone?'

136

'You can't just come in 'ere and...' one of the butchers began, but I didn't wait. I pushed through swing doors to the room at the back where another man was hacking into the side of a pig.

'Police!' I called. 'I need to phone the police.'

I spotted a payphone on the wall, grabbed the receiver and, looking around breathlessly, I punched in 999.

'Police, please.' I waited. 'Police? High Street. Flat 37B. Someone's dead, I think.'

'And your name, sir?' The operator asked calmly.

'Someone's dead, please, hurry.' I said again, and put the phone down.

*

'You've known the deceased long, sir?' The detective constable asked after they'd removed the body.

'No. No. Never met him.'

'But you knew he was dead?'

'It was the smell. What happened?'

'Too early to tell, really sir, but looks like he tried to take his own life.'

'Good God. How?'

'He had a gas oven in his room. Closed the windows, stuffed paper under the door, turned it on, but didn't light it. Then stuck his head inside.'

'I don't understand. I thought gas wasn't deadly.'

'Asphyxiated, according to the pathologist. The methane displaced all the oxygen in the room.'

'But why did he..?'

137

'You say, you didn't know him, sir?'

'No, I'd just arrived. Number 37A, one floor below. Do we know why he'd want to kill himself?'

'It happens, sir. People get lonely and depressed.

'You said he *tried* to commit suicide?'

'Looks like he stuck his head in the oven, changed his mind, panicked, and as he tried to extricate himself, he struck his head on the rim of the oven door and collapsed. Out for the count. It was only a matter of time before he slipped into unconsciousness and died. Mind you...' The detective looked solemnly at me. 'It's just as well you didn't open the door. If you'd gone in and switched on a light, the explosion would have taken out the whole street.'

'Good God.' I hesitated. 'And, the smell? That wasn't the gas, was it?'

'He died last Saturday, so the boys at the lab reckon. Flies don't hang around. Withing a couple of hours and they'd have located the corpse. The heat and humidity didn't help. Surprised no one noticed before.'

'I think everyone put the smell down to drains or the butcher's shop. Mrs Reardon - she lives up on the top floor - she reckons he was a loner. Kept himself to himself.'

'No friends, relatives?'

'A brother, I think. Came to see him last week.'

'He was odd.' It was Mrs Reardon. I wasn't sure how long she'd been standing there. 'It's a shame, though,' she said, 'him being dead an' that, but he was a most peculiar man.'

'Hello, Sis?'

'Where are you? You ok? We've been worried sick about you.'

'It's a long story.'

'But, you're OK?'

'Yes. I'm fine. I wonder…is that spare room still on offer? Just for a couple of weeks, 'til I get back on my feet. I'll pull my weight, hand over my dole money, keep the house clean, empty the rubbish, make sure the drains are clear…'

'Stay as long as you like. I'll make the bed and rustle up your favourite for this evening's meal. What would you like? Steak? Liver and bacon? Lamb's heart?'

'Couldn't have a salad, could I? Not sure I could face meat, not after…Oh, and chips, a large plate of chips.'

The 'Sophisticated' Englishman

Ian Patrick

They say that travel broadens the mind. There are some exceptions to this, of course, as demonstrated when, on the first full day of their holiday to Spain, Norm and Ethel are visiting the local market. Norm is a xenophobic Englishman and proudly displays either his Union Jack or his St. George's cross vests, when he is abroad. The vest displays his large flabby biceps that match an equally gross corporation. His wife, in contrast is a small, rather nervous, lady.

'Have you been served yet Ethel?'

He elbows his way to the front of the queue.

'Hoy. *Garçon.*'

There is no response.

'Hoy. Do you want my custom or not?'

The stallholder moves towards him.

'*¿Qué?*'

'Apples, I want some apples.'

'*¿Qué?*'

 He points towards the apples.

'Ah, *manzanas.*'

'No, I don't want manzanas, I want bloody apples.'

A helpful bystander says, 'The Spanish for apples is *manzanas.*'

'That's bloody stupid. Everybody knows that it's A for apple so why are they trying to change the language?'

'¿*Cuanto*?'

'What does he want now?'

The bystander raises his eyes impatiently.

'He wants to know how many.'

'How many apples do you want Ethel?'

'One.'

He indicates with his finger.

'¿*Quiere algo más*?'

'Do you want anything else?'

'Do you want anything else Ethel?'

'Bananas.'

'Ah, *platanos*.'

'No, are you deaf, I want ban-an-as.'

'¿*Cuanto? Uno? Dos*?' The stallholder holds up his fingers.

'How many, Ethel?'

'Two.'

Norm puts up two fingers. The stallholder would like to reciprocate.

'¿*Todo*?'

'Is that all?'

'Do you want anything else Ethel?' She shakes her head.

'No.'

'Dos euros.' This time the stallholder does hold up two fingers.

'Two euros, Ethel.'

He hands the money across.

'We have to support these poor Spaniards. They haven't two halfpennies to rub together.'

The helpful bystander puts in his two pennyworth, 'It'll be a long time before they get rich if they have to rely on the likes of you…'

141

'You've just got to be firm with these foreigners, Ethel. They don't seem to be able to take it in unless you shout at them. Look, this looks like a nice bar. Fancy a coffee or a beer or something?'

They sit down outside the bar.

After a few minutes, during which time Norm is becoming impatient, the waiter comes out.

'A pint and a coffee for the missus.'

'*Sí, una cerveza y un café.*'

'What the hell is he on about? I know I'm in a bloody café and if he brings me this cerveza rubbish instead of beer, he can take it back.'

The waiter goes off. He's seen this before and could guess what they are wanting. He comes back with a large beer and a cup of black coffee. He has anticipated the fact that the coffee needs to be white and holds the milk jug over the cup.

'*¿Con leche, señora?*'

Ethel gets the meaning and replies in the affirmative.

The waiter puts down two dishes of *tapas*.

'We didn't order food,' says Norm. 'You've made a mistake.'

'*Es gratis.*'

'Never heard of it. What sort of food is gratis? Anyway you can take it away. We don't want it.'

'*No, es gratis* – is free.'

'Free? Oh well that's different. Are you going to try some Ethel? I'll tell you what, it's not bad is this *gratis*. We'll have to order some more of this.'

He drinks the rest of his beer, gives a loud burp and summons over the waiter.

'Another beer and we'll have some more of this *gratis*. Are you having anything else, Ethel?'

Ethel says that she will have another coffee.

The waiter returns with the order including the *tapas*.

'This is different *gratis*. There must be more than one type of *gratis*. It makes it bloody difficult to order. I wonder why the hell they don't give the different types of gratis different names?'

They finish their drinks and the waiter is nowhere to be seen.

'There's no sign of the waiter and he's forgotten to charge us for the drinks. Quick let's slope off before he remembers.'

Half way along the street they hear a voice.

'*Señor*.'

They stop.

'*Señor, no ha pagado*.'

'I think he wants his money, Norm.'

'We thought you'd gone home,' quips Norm, as he hands over ten euros. 'Keep the change.'

'I don't know how they make a living, giving away free food with the drinks,' wonders Ethel.

They drive back towards the coast.

'Look at that idiot. Why the hell is he flashing his lights?'

'Norm. I think you're on the wrong side of the road.'

'Like, Hell. I'm on the *right* side. It's all these foreigners that drive on the *wrong* side. All right, all right, I'm moving over. Why the hell are they so damned impatient? If they didn't all stop work for a fiesta every day, they'd be able to take their time. A fine mess England would be in if we stopped work for a *fiesta* every afternoon. You can see them all in the bars on an afternoon and then they go back to work half canned. No wonder Spain's in a mess. Oh Hell, there's another one behind me now flashing its lights. Well he's not getting past me that's for sure. What Ethel? It says *Guardia Civil* on the bonnet. Don't worry. Seville's miles away from here so they must just be in a hurry. I suppose I'd better let them get past.'

'They want you to pull over, Norm.'

'Well, that was an expensive day out. One hundred and fifty euros that cost me. They said I was going too fast. I thought you could go one hundred and forty in Spain, but they said that even on motorways, that was too fast. I think they make up their own rules to catch out the holiday makers.'

'Well, he was nice and polite Norm and I liked his uniform.'

'I'd be bloody polite if I was taking one hundred and fifty euros from someone.'

'That was a nice place Ethel, but there's one thing I didn't like about it. There were too many English people there and I came on holiday to integrate with the natives. Now that we're learning the lingo, perhaps tomorrow we'll go to that village on the hill that they told us about on the bus from the airport. Bédar, I think it's called. Maybe we can find a nice bar there and get some more of that *gratis*.'

144

Almería - in search of a dream

Jane Breay

We are often asked how we ended up in what is, after all, a part of Spain still largely undiscovered by the British and indeed how on earth we came by the location for our house. So here it is: a story, which I am sure is echoed by many of our local expatriate friends and acquaintances.

For as long as I can remember, I had harboured a dream of early retirement to the peace and tranquillity of southwest France, at least for the winter. A two-week holiday in October 1998 put paid to the dream - poor weather and expensive food finally triumphed over rampant francophilia and I was prepared to concede defeat. My husband, who had shared my enjoyment of French holidays but not my enthusiasm for something more permanent, heaved a sigh of relief as we returned to tend our stunning if rather soggy Worcestershire patch.

Then a chance meeting on the boat opened new vistas. I was explaining my disappointment to an English couple who responded, 'But have you considered Spain?'

Unwelcome visions of various Costas, visited and unvisited but to be honest based more on prejudice than experience, filled my head and I tried to hide my scepticism as I tactfully explained that really we liked SPACE and open country.

'That's what you get in Almería', they responded. 'We live near Mojácar. The sun shines pretty well every day …the cost of living is ridiculously low…the locals are friendly and helpful…there is a thriving and well integrated expat community from all over the world in the little village of Bédar…'

That evening to my astonishment Terry announced that 'perhaps we should go and have a look.' I needed no further prompting, but clearing diaries proved a bit of a challenge - it's amazing how many things you are committed to when retired. Finally a date was found in late January when we could manage a week; enough for an exploratory visit and nothing lost if we didn't like it. In the meantime, some research was called for. Not for nothing, I realised, is Almería referred to as 'undiscovered Spain'. The city of Almería and the majestic Cabo de Gata, together with Mini-Hollywood and the town of Nijar rated between them just over a page out of over 400 in the Michelin Green Guide, whereas Mojácar itself got only nine lines. Even guide books devoted exclusively to the Andalucía region didn't offer much more.

Being undiscovered of course also meant being somewhat under-developed in terms of tourism/hotels - there was virtually nothing on offer in the main holiday brochures for the very good reason that package holiday accommodation did not exist. There were however good and reasonably priced *hostals* and expatriates were starting to open their homes and do B&B. This was to prove very

146

useful when looking to buy as the hosts had invariably been through the experience and were happy to share their knowledge and contacts.

Viewed from the air, the impression of Almería that greeted us was rather unprepossessing. The impression was of acres of plastic growing enough vegetables to feed the entire world. But 15 minutes north of the airport we left the plastic behind and entered an extraordinary landscape, as the motorway cut through mountains and traversed deep gorges. The geology of the area seemed very disturbed, the different strata in the rock, both vertical and horizontal, showing up in sharp contrasts of colour, ranging from ochre through olive green, grey, terracotta and even purple. Under a dazzling blue sky it had a rugged, uncompromising beauty, and initial shock gave way to fascination and our misgivings turned to enchantment as we spent a week exploring both the coast and the stunning mountainous hinterland with its own peculiar, savage beauty.

At first we were puzzled by the huge, dry riverbeds. We understood that rainfall could be as little as 5" a year, so why these enormous waterless watercourses? The simple answer, as we are only too aware 15 years on, is that when it does rain it REALLY RAINS and even these enormous beds are sometimes not enough to contain it, as we witnessed as recently as 2012.

Mojácar Playa was quite a different place in 1999 from the one we know in 2014, as there were few apartment blocks and much of the area beside the *paseo* was undeveloped. But even now that the developers have turned most of the land into apartment blocks, it still doesn't look like those Costas that I was so keen to avoid since nothing is high rise. Fish and Chips, garish souvenir shops and kiss-me-quick hats remain conspicuous only by their absence, and the largest shop along the beach is still the *Ferreteria* Lopez, although in its present incarnation several times larger than it was in 1999. Comfortingly it remains a veritable treasure trove, an eccentric mix of everything you could possibly want in ironmongery, small household and garden items. In the winter Mojácar is still as quiet as it was then, but now there seem to be more different nationalities, and in particular, increasing numbers of French visitors.

The narrow streets and glistening white houses of Mojácar Pueblo have not changed at all and nor has the view to the north - the extraordinary plain where it appears as if a giant digger has deposited huge pyramidal mounds, interspersed with houses, stretches of barren terrain and cultivated fields.

We explored all this during our week's stay, as well as Turre, Cortijo Grande and Vera, followed by Villaricos and San Juan de los Terreros to the north and as far south as Roquetas.

But our hearts were in the hills. We had fallen irrevocably in love with Bédar, a thriving community with small supermarket, bank, chemist, baker and four bars/restaurants where a warm welcome was always waiting and a cosmopolitan mix of ex-pats well integrated with the locals.

What's not to love?

So in the space of one short week we made the truly life-changing (and as it turned out, life-enhancing) decision to buy a property in or close to Bédar. Needless to say we were impatient to get started, so March found us back here.

It didn't take long to work out that there was not much for sale – apparently people who move to Bédar tend to stay. We were prepared to consider restoration or even building from scratch, although we were only too aware that the restoration route would involve a more or less open cheque and that building from scratch was likely to be an extremely long-winded process because of the difficulty of getting permission to build on rustic land.

We hit the ground running and saw enough to make our heads spin – from half-habitable village houses to old *cortijos* with not much more than a wall standing, to huge tracts of land with no electricity, water or planning consent.

Time, as ever, was the enemy – five days of our week had evaporated and we had seen nothing which truly captured our imagination. Then, on our final afternoon, our agent drove us a hundred metres or so down a bumpy track, rounded a bend between two small hills and stopped. The sun, which had been in hiding for the better part of three days, emerged from behind a cloud and lit up the landscape. Terry and I climbed out of the car in silence. The air was heavy with the scent of rosemary, lavender and thyme and the only sounds were the breeze in the pines, the song of the birds and buzzing bees. Jacqueline smiled smugly, like an indulgent parent on Christmas Day. She had learned a lot about us in five days and had evidently saved the best till last, confident that we could not fail to be captivated.

Spread out before us were many terraces, sparsely cultivated with almonds and the occasional olive, and pine-clad hillsides rising as much as a couple of hundred feet. Most of the terraces were south and southwest facing with wonderful views of distant mountains. ''Er…how much of this is included?' we enquired. 'Pretty well everything you can see – a total of over four hectares. There is no electricity nearby, or water, and you would need full planning consent. But there is plenty of land for more than one house and the vendor will only sell it as one piece, so perhaps you could sell on one part to help recover some of your costs…'

This sort of acreage had not figured in our plans and evidently some serious re-thinking of our strategy would be called for: clearly one does not build a two-bedroom winter home on a ten-acre plot which requires the expensive addition of all services, not to mention year-round attention to crops and gardens. Could it be that my dream of running a small B&B in a beautiful, warm setting might eventually become a reality? The area is popular with walkers and bird-watchers and the right place would surely enjoy year-round business. Terry began to fantasise about creating a wild-life friendly environment. We were, in short, well and truly hooked and my frustration knew no bounds as we went about our normal lives until our next opportunity to visit, which would not be until May.

During that time we agreed by phone and fax to buy the land subject to planning consent. I would like to say that the rest is history and indeed it is, but what a history! The easy bit was now behind us and I often had cause to reflect that when Nietzsche said 'What does not kill me makes me stronger' he'd obviously never tried building a home in Spain. During the following eight years we bought an apartment in Mojácar to have a base while we pushed things along, sold our property in England, bought a 'project' to keep Terry busy while architects, local authorities, Sevillana, Galasa and ultimately builders dragged their feet and we nipped at their heels until eventually, triumphantly, in 2007 we moved into Finca la Serenidad which is where we now continue to enjoy our Spanish adventure.

Would we do anything differently?

Very unlikely (well perhaps the odd, unimportant detail). Do we miss anything? Perhaps: raspberries, rhubarb and damsons, all of which we had in abundance in our English garden. What about the family? We get real quality time when they visit for a week or more, so even if we don't see them as often as we might have done back home, the time we do get is precious and all the more enjoyable. Have we ever regretted the decision to move here? Would we return to UK?

On both counts, resoundingly, NO!

A Sense of Duty

Ed Harvey

When I went to the police station and handed in a package I'd found on the train, it didn't occur to me that I was doing anything other than what any decent, law-abiding person would do.

I'd left work early and planned an evening in - a takeaway, something recorded, and a glass or three of Rioja.

Miraculously, I managed to find a seat on the five-thirty from Victoria and the journey was largely uneventful until Clapham when, as the tide of commuters washed in and out of the carriage, I noticed a package under a seat.

I was suspicious, of course. Any package on the five-thirty is suspicious, especially one wrapped in brown paper. At first, I assumed it must belong to someone, but it was under a seat that was unoccupied and I felt guilty, suddenly, as if *I'd* planted it there.

I looked round, wondering if anyone else had noticed it, but everyone seemed buried in their newspaper, smart phone, or just staring out of the window.

Quite uncharacteristically, I felt the urge to scream…

There's a package, under a seat!

Then, inexplicably (and, in hindsight, probably quite stupidly) I picked it up and turned it over, hoping to find an address or something else that might help to identify its owner.

I shook it - as I often did presents at Christmas – then placed it in my bag, carried it off the train, and stood on the forecourt, trying to remember the location of the police station...

'So, you found it on a train?'

I could tell the Duty Sergeant wasn't convinced.

First, he held the package at arm's length, as if it was radioactive, and then he passed it to a junior officer to x-ray, but it wasn't until he invited me into a room down the corridor that I realized I might not get home in time to have *an evening in*.

'Empty your handbag.'

'Pardon?'

'Handbag.'

'I'll just make a call,' I said, taking out my mobile.

'Solicitor?'

'Friend. We share a flat. Ask her to order a takeaway.' I hesitated...'Why, do I need one?'

'A solicitor?'

'Yes.'

'Depends.'

I phoned Sam.

'It's me. I'm at the police station. No, I haven't been arrested. They're x-raying a package I found on the five-thirty from Victoria. Yes, the five-thirty. I actually got a seat...'

A technician stuck a cotton-bud in my mouth, wiggled it about, and then took finger and palm prints from both hands.

'They're processing me. DNA, fingerprints. Eliminate me from their enquiries…You're right, I watch too much TV. Do us a favour? Phone and order numbers 12, 37 and 65. Ask them to deliver in about an hour. Thanks.'

I handed my mobile to the Sergeant. He slid a form in front of me and I signed it, but it wasn't until he followed the technician out of the cell that I realized I was alone and that both the door to my cell and the observation window were closed.

My cell? Wait a minute….

'Hallo,' I called, and banged on the door. 'I think there's been a mistake. Hallo. Is anyone there?'

I sat on my bunk. *My bunk?*

An hour later, a key turning in the lock woke me up.

'This way,' the duty Sergeant said, rather gruffly I thought.

'Look,' I said, 'the takeaway. It'll be delivered soon. I'd better get home.'

He didn't say anything, led me down the corridor and knocked on a door.

Three men sat behind a large desk.

'The suspect, Sir.'

The what? Now, just you…

'Recognize this?' one of the men said.

Well, of course I did. *It was my package. When I say my package, I mean…*

'The five-thirty from Victoria?'

'Yes.' I'd found my voice. 'Under a seat.'

'You know what's in it?'

'No, of course not. I brought it straight here. I thought, you know, it was the right thing to do.'

'Very public spirited.'

That was sarcasm; if ever I'd heard it. *Bloody cheek.*

They conferred and I waited.

'OK. You're free to go.'

I must have looked stupid, because he said it again.

I stood up. And then sat down. 'Not before I know what's in it,' I said. *Now who was being cheeky*? But I couldn't go, not without knowing. I'd spend the rest of my life wondering if it contained something unusual like a loved-one's ashes, false teeth, or glass eyes, or something mundane like a packed lunch.

I felt hungry suddenly.

They conferred again.

'What I'm about to tell you is highly confidential, do you understand?'

I nodded.

'You've been part of an experiment.'

I lent forward.

'You'll appreciate, with Christmas round the corner, that security on public transport is one of our highest priorities. We're evaluating the public's response to situations and measuring reaction times when an alarm is triggered.'

'Just a minute,' I said. 'What was I supposed to do? Pull the communication cord or run down the platform shouting, look out there's a bomb?'

155

'Did I say it was a bomb?'

'No, I just assumed…'

They conferred. AGAIN.

'You're right, it was a bomb.'

'Oh, my God.'

'A dummy, but real enough for our purposes.'

'But what if I'd panicked, screamed, *bomb, there's a bomb…*?'

'But you didn't did you?'

'No, I…'

'What should you have done?'

I smelt a rat...'I'm not sure.'

'Contact an employee?'

'What?' I snorted. 'Find a guard on a rush hour train?'

'On the platform, at the next stop?'

'By the time I'd got off and found someone, the train would've pulled out, and I'd be left stranded, pointing, mouth open…Not that easy, knowing what to do…'

'No, you're right. Next time, dial 999.'

'Next time?'

They conferred, yet again.

'Well, thank you for your cooperation. Your response has been most instructive.'

'That's it? No tea and biscuits?'

He smiled. 'We've contacted Sam. She'll delay the takeaway. A car will take you home.' He hesitated. 'Oh, and by the way…that form you signed? Official Secrets Act. You can't breath a word. Goodbye.'

Extranjeros

Mike Lightfoot

Those who haven't come to see
Our small white village might agree,
(While standing in Mojácar Square
And gazing at "that place up there"),
It looks an uneventful place,
A refuge from the frantic pace
Of life elsewhere. I disagree,
For Bédar, between you and me,
Is much the same as any place
That's peopled by the human race.

It has its share of artists, gays
And people who are writing plays,
The know-alls and the party spoilers,
Folk who know their way round boilers,
Cliques, the loners, hard of hearing,
Men who sport a diamond earring,
Snobs, the meek, the anorexic,
Children who can't spell dyslexic,
Star-crossed lovers, folk with boats,
Couples at each others' throats,
Piercings, purple hair, tattoos,
Alcoholics, drug abuse,
Hairy chests festooned with bling,
Caustic wits and those who 'sing',
Arguments and fierce vendettas,
Gossip, snubs and poisoned letters,
Boasters, chancers, cowards, heroes...
And that's just the *extranjeros*.

The Spanish are a different race
With different ways, a different pace.
They seem to lack a sense of time -
Punctuality, a crime.
They sleep at silly times of day,
Speak a "foreign kind of way" –
(Some say "goodbye" to mean "hello",
And why that's so we'll never know).
They come out when we're going home,
Not C of E, but Church of Rome,
They're communists, who *like* their King,
Their bureaucrats are maddening!
(God help you if you need a phone
Installing, for some faceless drone
Will ask you why you didn't know
You should have asked a year ago
On forms three hundred meters thick
In triplicate and Arabic).
They don't see how it can be fun
To go for walks without a gun,
And though we've been with them so long
Some still don't speak our native tongue!
Widows with their henna hair,
Bloody cyclists everywhere,
Workmen who arrive, then vanish -
But, before we knock the Spanish,
Stamp our feet and swear and cuss,
Remember - they put up with us!

The Cashier

Michael Palmer

Francisca had found time to reflect on her life in one of the few quiet moments in the Supermarket on the coastal strip, but there was no comfort in the hard plastic seat at the cashier's desk. Her bum was numb. Her legs were numb. In fact, her whole body felt numb. How many years had she had been sitting there? And for what? Certainly not the 'fun of the Costa Del Sun'.

Ouch! Standing up, Francisca tried to get some feeling back into her body. Although the relief was only temporary, it was better than nothing and, just as the feeling came back to her toes, a customer swayed into view. Sitting down again, her body moulded itself to the seat. How many customers had she served that hour, that day, that year? Each one expressed a range of emotions - resignation, urgency, frustration, or contentment.

Those who'd just got off the plane – pale and travel weary – were often unsure about what they were buying and would use up all the change from the till when they paid with a one hundred Euro note for milk, bread, wine and oil. And those she knew, who'd been here for years, she thought of as 'the sad ones'. They spoke to her in fluent Spanish, but now they too were alone, and confused and depressed about the future.

As the cash register sounded its electronic change of ownership, Francisca thought of the thousands of lives that passed her counter.

Where did they go?

Anywhere, would be more interesting than here.

She wondered what they thought of her? Perhaps, as a doorkeeper to some place of secular worship where the Gods extracted their dues and, having worshipped, they went on to fulfilled lives.

Eight a.m. saw her here, and eight p.m. would see her here still.

There were too many ties keeping her here and stopping her going out into the world. Perhaps it was too late to fulfil her dreams now. Dreams that were fading with the years with just the occasional flash of what might have been.

It seemed happiness was something everyone else was entitled to, but not her.

Oh, she'd had her moments, when her deep blue eyes would flash, her smile would dazzle and the movement of her body would entice…and when her body shook with laughter, it belied an inner charm. In times past, her body was curvaceous, her skin luminescent, her body language inviting and she'd been able to draw men to her like a siren…One, in particular…Juan.

A sudden 'bang' woke her from this musings. Not a customer, but a rep wanting an order.

'How are you Francisca?' asked Lopez.

'OK. And you?'

'Fine.'

She looked at the youth - the same age as her son - making his way in the world.

160

His inexperience of life allowed her to flatter him and he responded to the charm radiating from her. She knew he was confused, drawn like the fly to a Venus trap.

Lopez looked up and smiled the smile of innocence.

It amused her. She used her experience and knowledge of men to entertain herself and pass the time of day when she was bored. She wanted to know if her coquettish ways still worked and whether age, and her fuller, more matronly, figure could she still disturb them emotionally and bend them to her will.

'Well?' asked Lopez. 'How many cartons this week? We have a special offer.'

'How special?' This was business - time to work the magic and get a really good deal.

'10% off trade.'

'What? I can pay that price from *Mercadona*, as a customer.'

The rep shifted from one foot to the other and had obviously decided to try another tack…

'Well maybe another 5%. Make it 15%.'

Silence.

It was a game she played. The first to break the silence would be the loser.

Lopez appeared to mull over his options. He was a smooth operator and she knew he'd had a string of girlfriends to prove it. She imagined him wondering why this (slightly) overweight middle-aged lady was able to unsettle him and throw him off balance? He would be able to dismiss, or even ignore younger girls, but not me…he'd have to apply caution by the bucket load.

'OK. Make it 20%. Take delivery now. Cash. Deal?'

Francisca smiled. Victory was hers and, as an act of grace, she leant forward and kissed the rep on both cheeks.

He blushed and sauntered over to his van, lowered the tailgate and, after it had crashed to the pavement he guided a heavy cage full of goods through the entrance to the supermarket.

Francisca watched and imagined him thinking…'Soon have this sorted and be off and away.'

But, it was not to be…

Oh, yes, Francisca had told Juan not once, but a thousand times, to fix the hole at the entrance to the shop. 'And soon,' she'd said, 'before we have an accident.' Juan had shrugged a thousand times at the suggestion…perhaps one day, after he'd finished socialising with his friends or after golf...

The heavy cage lurched awkwardly and when its front castor hit the hole, it changed direction and headed straight for the storefront's plate glass window.

The more nimble customers scattered as the cage sped towards them. The less nimble stood, routed to the spot and prayed. And now, only one thing stood between the cage and the soon-to-be demolished window…Francisca's experience (reinforced by her mother) had taught her that there would be certain times in life when bold and decisive action would be required. For example, bold and decisive action would be required during any and every *relationship* - especially with men - and the sooner problems were ironed out, the better. Another instance when bold and decisive action would be required concerned *money*. The tighter the reign, the more you had, and the more you had, the less you needed worry about a 'rainy day'. And so with the benefit of her genetic make up and its application over the years, her mother's theory was about to put into action.

With the cage towering over and accelerating towards her, Francisca calmly picked up a heavy stick she kept close by in case of trouble and, when she jammed the stick into the front wheels, two things happened simultaneously.

The cage stopped dead and Lopez, who'd been trying to catch up with it, was taken completely by surprise, slamming into it and then thrown violently backwards onto the floor.

There was complete silence as everyone stared in shock at the poor boy who lay, if not actually unconscious, in a deeply dazed state.

After what seemed an age, clapping and shouting and sighs of relief broke the silence and Francisca was surrounded.

Juan pushed his way through the crowd, anxious to help (and check that his precious window was intact).

Lopez had a large bump on his head and, coming round, asked if he was in heaven.

'No, Lopez, you're not in heaven,' Juan said, 'but you knocked on the pearly gates!'

The Walk Home

Lesley Allen

Monsieur Bertrand pulled the door shut behind him and set off down the stone path leading to the lane. His was the last house in the village, or the first if coming from Narbonne.

The summer had been a favourable one, witnessed by the abundance of grapes hanging in large clusters from the vines surrounding his house. They stretched in military formation as far as the eye could see.

Monsieur Bertrand turned left at the empty house on the corner of the lane. The aged wooden shutters, bleached a pale blue by summer suns, stared like blinkered eyes down the street. Bygone echoes of children's laughter mingled with memories of long ago picnics on the lawn leading down to the River Aude. That was before Monsieur and Madame Thibault died and their children left to work in Lyon and beyond.

He crossed into the Rue de la Mairie, the flag of La Republique hanging motionless in the hushed calm of the day. The old men played dominoes on the wooden benches set round the fountain or dreamed of their yesterdays when young bones kept pace with young minds and everything was possible.

The bell rang out the quarter as he walked into the square, the pots of geraniums clustered on stone steps providing a walkway of colour as he made his way towards the *boulangerie*. The crisp brown bag containing two loaves of *pain de blé*, one round, the other long, were ready for him to collect on the counter. Madame Pelletier always wondered how a man on his own could eat that amount of bread every day. His order only varied on a Sunday when six miniature doughnuts filled with apricot jam were added to the bag. Standing in the light by the doorway reading a letter from her daughter Marietta now living in Angoulême, Madame Pelletier noted the approaching figure of Monsieur Bertrand. With the letter deposited in the copious pocket of her skirt she returned to the counter to await his arrival but the bell above the shop door remained silent. Returning to the doorway she saw him disappearing down the Avenue de St. Michel, the green cloth bag hanging empty from his arm. She shook her head in amazement. He always collected the bread at this time. Perhaps he had another appointment first? He was certainly walking faster than usual with the speed of a much younger man. Shrugging, she returned to her letter until the arrival of another customer could claim her attention.

With the polishing cloth in her hand, Eloise Martel saw Monsieur Bertrand pass in front of the window and smiled, but he didn't look in. During the war he had left the village along with her Father to fight with the Resistance, but had returned alone with the news of her Father's death.

He had died a hero, Monsieur Bertrand had told them. By his dying others were still alive to fight for freedom. He had never revealed the details fearing they would cause too much pain. Every year until her death, he had bought her Mother a small posy of flowers on the anniversary when others had long forgotten.

As he approached the last house in the village, or the first if you were coming from Homp, Monsieur Bertrand passed by the window of Lucie Dubois where she lay on the couch immobilised by her useless legs. The Latin inscription chiselled on an ancient stone embedded in the wall revealed this to have been a house of ill repute some two thousand years ago. A few in the village maintained that nothing had changed, for Lucie had never known the man who had fathered her. It was never spoken about, although she had grown up with the rumours that her Father was an alcoholic who had killed a man in a drunken brawl. Due to her disability, Lucie was unable to work and Madame Dubois laboured long hours in the houses of the rich to support them both. Every day Monsieur Bertrand left two loaves of *pan de blé*, one round, the other long on the table in the hallway, knocking on the door every Sunday morning to present her with a bag of doughnuts filled with apricot jam. He had always refused payment, saying that it was nothing, although sometimes it was all that came between them and hunger. Lucie wondered if he had left the bread this morning, as she hadn't heard the door open as usual.

Monsieur Bertrand continued to walk. A small black cat sat by the side of the lane washing itself. It didn't pause in its ablutions as he passed by. The blue of the River Aude glinted on his left and the last of the summer swallows sat on wires overhead. The road now petered out into a dusty track lined by thorny hedges of wild blackberries, and small clouds of midges swarmed in the long coarse grass that edged the lane.

A perfect late summer's day.

The stout figure of Madame Deniaud threw itself dramatically into the *boulangerie*. Her three chins wobbled as she tried to draw breath. She grasped the doorjamb for support - two large stains of perspiration shining wetly under the arms of her *chemisier*.

'Have you heard the news? Monsieur Bertrand had a heart attack last night! He died in the ambulance on the way to Narbonne!'

'*Non*!' Madame Pelletier cried, clutching her throat in consternation. She hurried to the shop doorway as if to recall the figure she had seen pass by. Catching sight of the bread still awaiting collection she superstitiously crossed herself.

Suddenly, the air was charged with the sound of the mourning bell lamenting the passing of one of its own. The swallows, startled by the noise, circled overhead before settling back on to the wires and the small black cat in the lane momentarily lifted its head before resuming its preening once more.

The Rugby Match

Doug Day

The changing room was much the same as many others I had used over the years, with a plain grey concrete floor, concrete block walls painted white, coat hooks screwed to wooden batons, and plain metal benches with wooden seating. The whole room was pretty morgue-like and by the look of my teammates - pale, red eyed - the look of confusion reinforced that description, and 'the living dead' came to mind.

It was the last day of our tour to the northeast, culminating in a Saturday afternoon match against a veteran's team from Durham. My team, 'The Pirates', was a veteran's team made up of players based in the Midlands, aged 35 to 55 years. We toured every year to a different part of the UK to play rugby against like-minded people. Our mission was to enjoy playing, to play to win, to enjoy the company, to drink hard and not to cause offence to anyone.

As I changed into my rugby kit, I looked around the changing room at my team mates. Team captain, Beaky, due to his 'Concordian' nose, sat on his own flicking through the match programme. Beaky sat in a corner, not because he had special status, but because he had severe flatulence that had fellow team members rushing for the exit. No one dared to light a fag in case the clubhouse exploded.

Big Mac, the tour organiser and manager, entered the changing room with glasses of sherry on a tray, a pre-match libation to settle the nerves and the stomach. Big Mac, a northern man, was a moaner and was at his most content when he had an audience he could bore to death, moaning about life in general. He should really have been called 'Metal Mickey' due to the number of metal plates in his body, as well as his two new knees and a hip.

'There'll be some ringers in the opposition team today,' he said. 'Their first XV have a cup match next week and want a run out to practice their moves. They've packed their Veteran's team with several young first team players. I've told them that's not in the spirit of the game, but it won't change things.'

'They're taking the piss. What a bunch of wankers,' said our hooker, Rubik, so named after the cube, which matched his build and, so some say, his intelligence.

'Precisely. It's not what we're about. We never have been, and never will be, cannon fodder for the benefit of others,' replied Big Mac.

He fixed us with a stare and the usual banter stopped, dentures were removed (to reveal gaps originally occupied by front teeth) and gum shields were inserted.

Things were about to get serious.

Players were applying miles of strapping tape to parts of their bodies such as knees ankles, wrists and fingers, as well as areas that would leave you staring in wonderment. And, ah…the smell of horse liniment and Deep Heat, mixed with flatulence and fag smoke. To anyone who has played rugby, this would be familiar, but for those of you who have never encountered the likes before, I'll leave your imagination to fill in the details.

Experience, in the modern era, is a dirty word - meaning *old and past it* - but it's worth a king's ransom in a game of rugby and our team was a mixture of former first-class players, County caps and the odd former International.

Time for the Captain's team talk.

'Right, all in,' demanded Beaky. We gathered round, intent on getting our team orders and game strategy. 'Twenty minutes to go and our last game. They've shown us no respect by putting first teamers in. Don't do anything silly and keep it tight because, if the opposition tackle us early in the game and turn over possession and score, it would be a travesty.'

Our prop, Sludge, an accountant by trade who found it difficult to appear tidy (people would give him their change when he was out, taking him for a vagrant) said, 'Skip, I was wondering, how many points do they get for a travesty?'

It was impossible not to laugh.

Beaky recognised the moment had gone. 'I'm going to do the toss.' He downed his sherry, stubbed out his fag on the concrete floor and left to find the referee and opposition captain.

The eloquent Holmes, a criminal lawyer, took over.

'Gentlemen, a toast.' We all grabbed a glass of sherry. 'Right, let's get going!'

'The Pirates!' we chorused and downed our sherries in one.

Thumper, our 5 foot 4 inch winger with big ears and large feet, was so carried away with the occasion that he hurled his empty glass at the wall. It smashed to pieces.

'You prat!' shouted Holmes. 'Who's going to clean that up? You're not Russian, drinking vodka.'

'Sorry. I got carried away. I've seen them do it on the telly,' said Thumper.

'Look around you,' Holmes said. 'A team of the finest men you could wish to meet.'

Salmon broke wind and Honkers, who was next to him, started to wretch.

'As I said,' Holmes continued, 'before me I see the finest of men, ready to go 'over the top' and never take a backward step.'

'Holmes, do shut up! You're not in court now. I'll be in tears before long,' said Watson, a giant from Gloucester and Holmes's best mate.

Beaky returned and we linked arms and formed a circle for the final warm up. We stomped in unison, our studs ringing on the concrete floor. It was a sound designed to terrify the opposition and the illusion was completed with aggressive shouting and kicking the metal kit cupboard.

In contrast to the energy displayed by our opposition (who were running out from the changing room and then passed a ball, stretched and generally looked quite healthy) ours was a slow, measured walk onto the pitch.

Rubik trotted over to the *Alicadoos* (non-playing tourists) and grabbed a fag. He insisted it was good

171

to have a cough before a game in order to open up the lungs.

It was a warm sunny afternoon. The pitch was huge, well grassed and dry - ominous conditions that meant the opposition could fly around and run us ragged.

Our plan was simple...Cheat!

Durham, our opposition, kicked off.

The ball came from the sky to Salmon.

'Mine,' he shouted, and leapt like his namesake travelling up river to spawn. Unfortunately the ball landed five foot away.

'Shit forgot to put my contact lenses in.'

As the front rows went down for the first scrum, Rubik belched (he liked *vindaloo*, extra chillies) and I saw his opposite number start to turn green. Sludge, the prop, introduced himself to his opposite number with a few well-chosen words: 'God you're ugly. What are you going to do for a face when Saddam wants his arse back?'

The scrum broke up with some pushing and shoving and I smiled. The plan was working: get them thinking about anything, other than rugby.

But Durham's first score came after a flowing move and the winger ran in unopposed.

'Where was Honkers?' cried Beaky. 'He should have tackled the wing.'

Meldrew (so called, because he was a miserable git) replied, 'He's throwing up in the hedge.'

We waited under the posts for the conversion to be taken as Honkers ran back on the pitch, his face bright pink from straining. 'What have I missed?'

The game restarted. The ref blew for a penalty after Thumper felled the winger.

'What's that for?' demanded Thumper.

'Late tackle,' the ref replied.

'It can't have been late, we've only been playing for two minutes!'

Using all of our experience, we slowed the game down, held onto the ball, and Durham's young, first team players became very frustrated. Things were not panning out as they'd planned. Us *old bastards* were not supposed to be *that* good but, just before half time, Durham managed to score another try. On this occasion, it was the sheer pace of their centre that left The Pirates for dead.

Fourteen points down.

Then the relief of half time.

It was traditional for half-pints of Guinness to accompany the water and oranges and a packet of fags for those who felt in need.

I grabbed a Guinness and said to Rubik, 'Shit. I've stopped sweating. Need more fluid.'

Taking a long drag on his fag, Rubik looked at me and replied, 'In order to sweat, a modicum of exercise is required. Need I say more?'

Big Mac called us together. 'Well done lads. We're getting to them. They're starting to whinge. Just keep it tight, make no mistakes, and bore the pants off them.'

The second half followed a similar pattern to the first: slow and easy. Durham had a lineout near their try-line following an inch-perfect kick by Beaky. Surprisingly, we won the lineout (I realised how when I saw Watson standing on the foot of the

Durham jumper) and, as a result, we managed to score a converted try.

Fourteen points to seven.

Beaky kept up a barrage of comments aimed at the referee.

'Look,' said the ref, 'whose reffing the match, me or you?'

'That's the problem. Neither of us,' replied Beaky.

Frustration was building within the ranks of the opposition first team players as we niggled away at them Durham threw the odd punch for good measure. Still, we remained disciplined and kept tactics to suit us, but then something happened that changed the whole nature of the game.

The opposition overstepped the mark.

There was a ruck (a posh word for lots of bodies grappling for the ball on the floor). It broke up and our wing, Thumper, was left lying on the floor. He'd been knocked out. His right eye was closing fast and there was reddening round his right temple.

This had been no accident.

Thumper came round gradually and was taken from the field, but his 'accident' left a sour taste in our mouths…Veteran's rugby is about enjoyment, a chance to share golden days with your opposition…

Holmes asked, 'Did anyone see what happened?'

Beaky replied, 'A cheap shot by their number 6 whilst Thumper was pinned down.'

I looked across at the opposition.

I saw their number 6 demonstrating the punch to his teammates, but the most annoying aspect of this display was the smile he had on his face.

The Durham captain came over. 'I'm sorry,' he said, 'that should never have happened.'

'These things happen,' Holmes shrugged.

He waited until their captain was out of earshot and then turned to me. 'Plod (my tour name) next scrum, start it off.'

The next scrum duly arrived and the front rows engaged.

'I love you,' I said to my opposite prop, with as much sincerity as I could muster. I kissed his cheek and then stuck my tongue in his ear. He erupted with rage and the whole scrum stood up - handbags at dawn. The referee was running around, blowing his whistle, trying to restore order and the next thing I saw was their number 6 running off the pitch as if the four horsemen were chasing hm. He pushed past spectators and went straight to the changing rooms.

Holmes and Watson had dissolved with laughter.

'What did you do to him?' I asked.

'When the trainer was on the pitch, sorting Thumper out,' Holmes said, 'I got the Deep Heat out of his bag and squirted a load into my pocket. Next breakdown at the scrum, Watson grabbed the number 6 and held him while I dipped my hand into the Deep Heat. I put my hand down the front of the number six's shorts and wiped the Deep Heat all over his balls. I reckon he could beat Usain Bolt with the speed he left the field!'

The game ended. An honourable draw, contrived by the opposition by way of an apology for what had happened and for not honouring the spirit of a veterans' fixture.

In the clubhouse afterwards, as the drink flowed, Holmes gave a rendition of '*Balls on Fire*' to the well-known tune, '*Wheels on Fire*'. Oddly enough, the opposition number 6 was nowhere to be found and I had visions of him dangling his tackle in a bucket of ice.

Who said age and experience has no place in modern life?

The Aristocratic Arrival

Lyn McCulloch

Pedro and Berto watched lazily from their place in the shade under the neatly clipped laurel tree as the big silver car drew into the Plaza de la Constitución. It was another hot, hot day and they'd been for their walk early so that the rest of the day could be idled away watching the world go by. They'd already noted several of the expat community in their skimpy shorts and vests heading out in their cars, presumably going to the beach. The Spaniards were more sensible, keeping out of the sun and riding out the heatwave.

As the car stopped a man and a woman got out and started to unload the luggage. There was plenty of it; they were obviously staying a while.

Pedro turned to Berto. 'It's the Princess, isn't it?'

Each year the Princess came to stay. She swept in, bringing a touch of glamour to the small white village, and the locals were agog to see how she looked, and whether she'd favour them with a glance or go straight into the big white house which took up the whole of one side of the square.

Her flunkies were still unloading bags and the accoutrements of her stay. She even brought her own food, they noticed, as several containers of exotic snacks were carried in.

Pedro and Berto had seen all this before. They knew the routine. Once everything was ready, the Princess would emerge from the back of the car, beautifully coiffed and sporting the latest accessories. They waited with bated breath to see if she would look their way.

Slowly they struggled to their feet and stretched, straightening up and strolling nonchalantly towards the car, hesitating some way away, waiting to see whether their presence was welcome.

The man opened the back door and she emerged in one elegant movement. She stopped and looked around, ignoring both Pedro and Berto who, forgetting himself, had taken one step towards her.

'Come on, Fifi.' A pink lead was clipped onto to a silver diamante-studded dog collar and the couple led their small French poodle, into the house. She didn't even give Pedro or Berto a fleeting glance.

They sighed and returned to their place next to the bench under the tree. Maybe tomorrow she'd acknowledge them, but they didn't hold out much hope. They'd never even been brushed and Pedro had only half an ear on one side, following a nasty altercation with a cat as a pup.

They just weren't in her league. They closed their eyes and went back to sleep, their excitement over for the day.

Powder Games

Jane Breay

Lucy jogged along the deserted beach. It was hard running close to the sea because her feet kept sinking into the wet sand, so she stayed near the promenade. It felt good to be exercising again after her convalescence. The burst appendix had been a blessing in disguise; she had been in need of some relief from the stresses of work.

There were no shops here, just a couple of bars on the beach, with evidence of preparation going on for the Easter holiday. Most of the villas on the other side of the promenade looked as though they could do with a good coat of paint and the whole area had the appearance of an abandoned movie set.

She was nearly at the far end of the beach when the wind began to whip up the sand, stinging her bare legs and her face. Screwing up her eyes, she turned to run back alongside the houses.

As the light faded, enormous drops of rain began to fall, not many to start with but soon gathering pace. She clearly could not outrun the storm and needed to find shelter or she would be soaked in no time.

The garden walls were low enough to vault and most of the houses had covered terraces. She selected one with some tatty furniture, so she had a grandstand seat to watch the spectacular storm. Great claps of thunder sounded overhead and huge streaks of lightning lit up the afternoon sky, which was now as dark as midnight.

The darkness had an eerie quality and Lucy found the sound of palm trees being tossed by the wind rather unsettling. Then among the swishing of the leaves and the creaking of the branches she heard another sound – a scrabbling, which seemed to be coming from inside the house.

There were no lights, the garden was completely overgrown - no sign the house had been inhabited in many months. So what on earth..?

The windows had wrought iron security grilles, so the only way in would be the door behind her.

Lucy waited several seconds, listening until she heard it again.

She knocked and called out…

'*Hola. ¿Permiso?*' Can I come in?

The scrabbling paused briefly and then resumed more frantically, accompanied by a pitiful cry, almost like a baby.

That did it. Time for Lucy the holidaymaker to give way to Lucy the intrepid investigative journalist.

She tried the door and to her surprise it swung open and out shot a tiny kitten. He didn't hang around to express his gratitude but made off at top speed in the pouring rain. Lucy let out her breath and laughed, releasing the tension.

The porch was open on two sides and no longer offered much shelter from the wind and rain which by now were whipping round from all directions, so she decided to take advantage of the refuge offered by the house.

She found a light switch just inside the door, but the power seemed to be off. However there was a half-open blind to the right, allowing the intermittent flashes to illuminate the interior.

She was in a large open plan living area. In front of her were a couple of sofas and a coffee table with several beer cans, some candles and the remains of a meal. With the next flash she glimpsed a kitchen to the right, beyond a dining area. Lucy blinked and focused her gaze on the breakfast bar while she waited for the next flash. When it came it was the brightest yet and clearly confirmed what she thought she had glimpsed: a scatter of small clear packets, some digital scales, a scattering of white powder, a bottle of something which could be white spirit.

Without considering the consequences of discovery, she crossed the room to investigate. One cupboard was crammed with boxes of the little packets and in another were several bags of bicarbonate of soda.

No doubt about it: a drug dealer's den.

She took her phone out of her bum bag and was considering who to call when she saw headlights pulling up outside and heard the slam of two car doors. A sharp pull told her the back door from the kitchen was locked. No escape that way. She ducked below the breakfast bar and flattened herself against the cupboards.

As the steps reached the door she heard a voice ask in Spanish,

'Did you leave this door open?'

'Definitely not.'

'Then we've had visitors. Check upstairs. I'll get this bedroom.'

One set of footsteps headed to a door behind the sofas and another up the stairs, then they called out to one another that there was no one in the house. Lucy was relieved that she could follow everything despite the pronounced Andalucían accents.

'Well there's nothing we can do now. Maybe we didn't shut it properly.'

A phone rang.

'*Hola Hassan. Sí, soy Diego ¿Qué tal?*

'When do you dock?'

Pause.

'Good, that'll fit really well.

'Paco's got himself a fake HGV license. We found a driver willing to let us use his lorry for a fee but he doesn't want to be in the vehicle with the goods in case he gets caught. So he's agreed that we tie him up and leave him after he picks up his last load this evening at about ten. He'll stop for a break at his usual bar and we can do it there. That should get Paco to the port just before midnight.

'Just a minute, he's got the details.'

A brief pause, then the second man spoke.

'Hi, Hassan. The lorry windshield has the names Pedro y Maria across the top, registration number 7426 CFM.

'We'll text you if there's any delay otherwise I'll be there just before midnight. It should be simple for you to put the packages in the cab while I'm unloading.'

Lucy knew that unless they left straightaway it wouldn't be long before she was discovered. While they were talking she had managed to activate the GPS tracker on her phone and was contemplating the best place to hide it when it rang. She cursed inwardly as she switched it off.

A face appeared round the counter and she was pulled roughly to her feet.

'*¿Quién demonios eres?*' Who the hell are you? Despite her fear, Lucy had the presence of mind to realise that it would be better if they didn't know she could speak Spanish.

'I don't understand,' she replied in English, struggling to escape Diego's grip. He took her phone and put it in his pocket and pulled her hands behind her back.

'Get some tape,' he told Paco.

Together they secured her hands and pushed her down on the sofa.

'So, pretty lady,' Diego said, in heavily accented English. 'Who are you? What you doing here?'

It wasn't hard for Lucy to look and sound terrified as she played the part of the innocent holidaymaker. She shook her head and stammered disjointedly. 'Nothing. Really. Nothing. I'm Lucy Dobson...I...I was jogging along the beach... sheltering from the rain...I heard a cry...a kitten behind the door. When it opened I thought it would be drier in here...'

The storm had pretty well blown itself out and it was too dark to see his features clearly, but she sensed him shaking his head, and then he grabbed her bum bag, opened it and took out her wallet and passport, which he studied by the light of a small torch.

'Ah, a journalist…not perhaps a holidaymaker. I don't think joggers hide. I ask again – what you doing here?'

Lucy shook her head dumbly. 'If you think I'm a burglar, why don't you call the police? My fiancé will be wondering where I am…'

Diego translated for Paco and added, 'Even if it's true about the fiancé, if he goes to the police it'll take a day before they do anything.'

'But she could identify us; shouldn't we get rid of her?'

'We'll deal with her tomorrow. Killing her here would leave evidence. We haven't got time this evening.'

Lucy was relieved that they seemed to have swallowed the notion that she had no Spanish and she could hear them conversing freely as they moved about. But she had no illusions about what was intended for her tomorrow.

'OK,' said Diego. 'Let's get this stuff into the car. We may as well go and eat - she'll be safe enough here till tomorrow if we tie her ankles and tell her we're coming back soon.'

'Let's gag her as well. I know there aren't many people around now but in the morning there could be.'

Lucy struggled futilely as they bound her ankles, stuffed a rag into her mouth and tied a cloth round her head. Diego told her they would be back in an hour and left, locking the door behind him.

A streetlight now illuminated the kitchen through the open blind. That would help in her search for the means to free herself, but her first challenge was to get to the kitchen. She soon abandoned bunny hopping; it would be too easy to crash face down on the tiles. The only way was on her tummy, drawing up her knees and extending her torso forward. It was agonisingly slow and she was soon sweating with the exertion.

Eventually she arrived at the breakfast bar. Without hands this was going to be tough. She manoeuvred herself into a sitting position against the kitchen wall, level with the end of the bar and, and gradually pushed herself upright.

She had a good view of all the surfaces and soon spotted what she was after – a knife rack.

Shuffling along with her back to the cabinets was easy compared with what she had already done. When she was level with the rack she found it quite a stretch to reach all the way across the counter to pull off the knives, despite her 5ft 9 inches. She selected a small, serrated one, pulling it off with her teeth and dropping it on the surface. Still using her teeth, she pulled open a drawer, inserted the knife with the blade outside, and closed the drawer on it as far as it would go.

Then she turned round, manoeuvred her hands until the bindings were level with the blade and started to saw, moving her body up and down. It was surprisingly easy and inside five minutes her hands were free, if a little scratched. She shook them to restore the circulation, cut the rope round her feet and removed the gag.

She spent a few minutes in a futile search for a key to the back door before it occurred to her that the ground floor bedroom would have French doors and that people tend to leave the keys in the room. She lit a candle and took it into the bedroom. Sure enough, there was a key in the lock of the French window.

One of the cuts on her hand was bleeding and she went into the bathroom to look for a plaster. She found a pack and as she washed her hands she surveyed herself in the mirror. A heart-shaped face with grey eyes, topped with a mass of dishevelled blonde curls and a mouth set in a determined line, stared back at her.

She fetched her bum bag with its contents from the living room, taking care in handling the passport, which would have Diego's prints. She added the tape she had cut from her wrists and which Paco had handled and made her escape.

As she ran back to her apartment she considered who, if anyone, to call. Certainly not the police, at least not yet; she didn't want to get tied up in red tape and miss the action. She tossed up between her boss, James, and her main contact at the Met, DS Steve Farrell, an old university friend, former lover, brother-substitute, occasional guardian angel and above all her best friend for nearly half her life.

Back at home she fired up her iPad to check the location of her phone tracker. It was stationary and not far away. There was a raft of emails and missed Skype calls from both of them. She was delighted that Steve's Skype button was live and James' wasn't.

'Hey Lucy, what gives? The big boss says you switched on your tracker and he can't get hold of you. He's climbing the walls.'

Lucy gave him a concise summary of her adventures, finishing with…'I'm looking at my tracker now. It's not moving.'

'I can see that. I'm not at work so I've had nothing better to do than watch it and worry for the last two hours! Have you any idea what lorry they might be talking about?'

'Only one obvious option. There are gypsum quarries a little way inland – someone told me that there's a fleet of over 300 lorries, sometimes working 24/7 bringing it to the port here in Garrucha. I think most of the drivers are independent operators so it's probably one of them.

'I imagine you're going to tell me to go to the Guardia Civil but I really don't want to do that yet – they'll keep me for hours on end and I'll lose the chance of a big scoop.

'On the other hand, if I don't tell them I could get into all sorts of trouble later on. Can you find out if they have an anonymous drugs hotline? That way I can give them the info and if they act on it I'll be able to be there when it all kicks off.'

'OK, I'll do that. But please do call them when you get it. You're an investigative reporter, not a policeman and this is hard-core stuff, not an exposé of a company with dubious ethics. If you want to do the other stuff you know the Met will have you any day!'

Lucy could see the concern in his voice reflected on his face and she recognised the unspoken subtext: if she didn't call the police, he would feel obliged to do it himself.

187

'The tracker's not far from here. I've found it on Street View. Looks like a little bar-restaurant…just swinging round…there's another bar on the other side of the road – very convenient. That's where I'm headed. I'm starving and it gets me into a good position if they move.'

'Lucy, please, no heroics…'

'I'll keep a low profile, I promise. I obviously haven't got a phone but I'll take my iPad and all the other toys with me – I'm sure James will be happy to pay the data roaming charges if I bring him a scoop. Can you contact him and let him know what's going on?

'I'll be in touch when I get to the bar.

'I'm soooo glad you convinced James to get me that tracker!'

Lucy logged off before Steve could make further protest and quickly changed into black jeans, t-shirt and leather jacket. She added a baseball cap which was all she could muster by way of disguise in case the dealers were sitting near the window and collected what Steve called her 'fearless investigative reporter equipment' - 'fire pack' for short. Following an assignment which had nearly ended badly, he had talked the paper into providing her with some top-notch technology to keep in touch.

The pack consisted of a mini iPad and a top of the range phone (both equipped with sophisticated tracking devices); a belt with a tracker in the buckle; a wireless mic/camera (which connected to either of these and could be remotely accessed by Steve or James); a tiny Bluetooth earpiece (which also networked to the iPad and the phone); and a powerful digital camera about the size of a matchbox. On the rare occasions she had used the whole kit she had felt as though she had strayed into an episode of a spy thriller.

The mic/camera looked like a classy piece of silver jewellery in the shape of a shell and could be worn on a chain or as a brooch. She slung it round her neck and checked that it was working with the iPad.

Steve had gone offline, leaving a message with the hotline number. She replied telling him that the mic/camera was switched on and she was wearing her earpiece and her tracker belt.

Clearly calling the police from her own phone would defeat the object of anonymity so she found a payphone and gave a synopsis of the relevant information. She omitted the bits relating to her imprisonment and finished by telling the operator where the dealers were currently located but emphasized that they would probably not have anything incriminating with them yet. The operator tried to persuade Lucy to tell her where the information came from and to meet one of their officers but she had no intention of letting anyone get in the way of her witnessing the bust.

The bar was busy enough that she would not draw attention to herself. She sat down in a corner facing the door, with a good view of the building opposite. She ordered a drink and some *tapas* and reconnected to find messages from Steve and James. The former wanted to know if she had contacted the police and the latter wished her luck and telling her to take care.

She replied to Steve, confirming she'd contacted the hotline and then for the first time since she had opened the door for the kitten, she found herself with time for proper reflection.

It didn't take her long to realise what Steve had already hinted at; that perhaps she was crossing a line? It was one thing to go undercover to expose questionable behaviour among care-home staff or sharp sales practices, but he was right that this was really police work.

What was driving her? Surely not just desire for revenge on the toe-rag who had every intention of disposing of her? She had neither the means nor the authority to arrest someone herself, so why put herself in danger when the story would be every bit as good if she could just be there for the bust?

Plus there was another much more important reason for doing it right. Steve was about to take up a promotion to Detective Inspector. She couldn't bear it if his position was compromised if it came out that he had been aware of the circumstances and had done nothing officially.

Before she had time to communicate with him, the tracker started to move and within seconds two figures emerged onto the pavement opposite. She settled her bill as the tracker moved round the corner and paused, presumably as they got into their car.

As soon as it moved off she left the bar, sprinted to her car and got underway, the tablet on the passenger seat showing the tracker gathering speed.

Her earpiece crackled into life.

'Can you hear me, Lucy?'

'Loud and clear. They're up ahead, in a dark green or blue four-wheel drive of some sort. A Merc I think. Must be them. There's no one else headed that way. I'll just get close enough to read the number.'

She gave Steve the registration, commenting that it was recent so they were probably not dealing with amateurs.

'Don't get too close if there's not much traffic - back off and let the tracker do the work. Your belt and your iPad trackers are on line now so if they get separated I will assume you're in trouble.'

'OK. We're turning right to leave the town. I guess we'll be heading towards Almería.'

As they covered the ten-minute drive to the motorway, Lucy took the opportunity to sort out the communications issue. 'Steve?'

'Yup.'

'I wouldn't want them to know that a Met officer had known about it if it goes pear-shaped. Can you get one of your Spanish-speaking colleagues to call the Spanish drugs people officially and give them a heads-up?'

'Good decision. I have Maria's number to hand. I'll brief her now.'

She could hear the relief in his voice.

'Thanks …'

It went quiet for a while and then Steve came back.

'Maria's calling now. She'll make them aware that the call to the hotline was yours so they should be able to connect the dots quickly.'

'We're just joining the motorway now, in the direction of Almería. They're observing the speed limit on the button.'

Then, a few minutes later…'OK. We're leaving the motorway in the direction of Sorbas.

'Lights up ahead on the left. Looks like a bar. They're pulling over into a car park with several lorries. I'm going to park further on and walk back,' she said as she rounded a bend and pulled over.

'Not a smart idea, Lucy. The tracker hasn't moved since they stopped, so either they're still in the car or they've left the phone there. Probably they're still there, waiting for the driver to come out. They won't want anyone in the bar to see them.'

'OK. I'll stay put till they move. There's an orange grove between here and the bar which would give me some cover.'

She opened the windows in case she could pick up any sounds, and as she leaned over to pick up her camera, an arm reached in and covered her mouth

'*¿Quién es, y que está haciendo aquí?*' Who are you and what are you doing here? 'I'm going to remove my hand and prove to you that I am a police officer,' the voice informed her in both Spanish and English.

She heard Steve frantically calling her name, asking what was going on as the police officer continued…'It's very important that you make no sound. Do you understand?'

Lucy nodded and the hand was removed and a warrant card in the name of Eduardo Gonzales of the *Brigada Central de Estupefacientes* was pushed under her nose, lit by a small torch.

Lucy breathed a sigh of relief. 'It's OK Steve – he's Drug Squad.'

She lapsed into Spanish.

'I'm Lucy Dobson. A journalist. Scotland Yard have been in touch with your office…I have a mic connected to an officer there.'

He answered his mobile, which must have been on vibrate. The conversation seemed to involve her. He hung up.

'You were the anonymous caller?'

Lucy nodded.

'Well it's a pity you didn't come directly to us – we nearly blew it.

'These are very dangerous people if cocaine is involved. I have officers stationed all around and you have to leave – I can't risk your safety.'

Lucy started to protest. 'If it weren't for me there would be no operation…'

'Señorita Dobson, I can't be responsible…'

'Please call me Lucy. You obviously speak English. Will you talk to a UK Drug Squad officer?'

Gonzales sighed.'OK, but this needs to be quick.'

He got into the car and Lucy addressed Steve.

'Officer Gonzales wants me to leave for my own safety. He speaks English. Please tell him I'm capable of looking after myself.'

'OK, but if he says you go, you go.'

She handed Gonzales her earpiece.

193

'He's Sergeant Steve Farrell.' She gestured to her pendant. 'Face me and the mic will pick you up.'

Gonzales listened in silence for two or three minutes, his eyebrows on occasion heading towards his hairline, then said, 'OK, I'll do what I can.'

He handed her back the earpiece for Steve to speak to her.

'He's agreed to let you witness some of the action and take photos if possible, without jeopardising the operation or your safety, but you have to cooperate. OK?'

'OK, thanks!'

'I hear you are stubborn and capable and that he has occasionally broken the rules for you,' said Gonzales. 'He told me about your imprisonment, which suggests you're pretty resourceful.

'But I need to formally warn you that this is a very dangerous situation, and as a civilian you should leave now. If you don't, you must do everything I tell you, but even so I can't be responsible for your safety.'

'I understand.'

He led her into the orange grove, where six officers were waiting. All were dressed in black, some in tracksuits and some in jeans and jackets and all had the same headphone mics as Gonzales. They eyed her warily as he explained her presence and introduced them by their Christian names.

He instructed two officers to return to their car, ready to follow the lorry to and from the port.

'When the driver leaves the port, the team stationed there will arrest any crew member who has been seen climbing into the cab, so you follow the lorry back.'

He indicated a second pair of officers.

'You go back to your car, too. If Diego leaves with the lorry driver, I'll let you know and you can follow. The rest of us will stay here and catch you up if necessary.

'With five of us in two cars we'll have enough people to follow them both if they split up, but our priority will be Diego not the driver. If it works well we'll all be back together for the bust.'

The two officers melted away into the trees and Gonzales said,

'OK let's get to the edge of the orange grove where we can see the bar. Lucy you can come but whatever happens you stay in the trees – they could easily be armed.'

They spread out, each officer sheltered by a tree, with Lucy slightly further back, just behind Gonzales.

He whispered to her...'We followed the driver here. His lorry's at the far end.'

Within a couple of minutes, several people exited the bar, bidding one another farewell, each climbing into his own cab. They were all clear of the area before the final one emerged.

Lucy's tracker moved as soon as he showed himself, and she saw two people leave the Merc and head towards him. The three exchanged some words, before Paco climbed into the cab and set off and Diego and the driver headed behind the building.

Gonzales spoke into his headset.

'Lorry's off to the port. The others are on foot. We don't need to keep too close. He still has the tracker. José and Carlos, stay in your car. He might still leave in the Merc.'

Lucy obediently stayed in the trees as Gonzales and the other officers followed Diego at a safe distance. Within a very short time Diego returned to the Merc alone but showed no sign of moving off.

The team returned to where Lucy was waiting.

'There's a broken down old building. He must have 'secured' the driver there,' Gonzales told her.

'It's going to be a long wait; an hour and a half plus unloading. Let's find somewhere to sit. It's not going to be comfortable but it's better than standing.'

They settled themselves as best they could and he quizzed her about what had happened at the house.

'Would you mind making a statement? I understand if you don't want to get involved by formally telling us about the kidnap, but we really need the statement about the drug paraphernalia to get a search warrant.'

They were speaking in Spanish and she could almost feel Steve's frustration. She translated for him and he predictably told her that as a policeman he would like the full statement because it would increase the jail time, but as her friend he didn't recommend it.

Lucy found Gonzales easy to talk to and enjoyed practising her Spanish. It didn't seem long before they heard from the port team that the lorry was on its way back and Hassan had been arrested without much fuss.

Lucy sensed an increase in tension as the minutes ticked away. One of the group by the bar had returned to his car to collect a searchlight and made his way stealthily round the back of the building, to be in a position to dazzle Diego through the windscreen when the group moved in. José and Carlos joined the group by the bar but Gonzales instructed those following the lorry to stay in their car when they got back in case Diego managed to drive off after the drop.

His headpiece suddenly crackled into life.

'Two kilometres away,' he announced.

Everyone stretched and readied themselves, drawing their weapons and checking them yet again.

Within seconds the lorry drew up; Paco jumped down from the cab with a large holdall and headed towards the Merc.

'Now!' said Gonzales. The car was suddenly brightly illuminated and officers seemed to Lucy to materialise from nowhere to surround Paco and the car just as he opened the door.

'Armed Police. Put your hands up.'

An engine roared into life and Lucy photographed the scene as the Merc moved off, knocking over the light and the officer behind. Paco sprinted towards the orange grove, pushing another one to the ground.

She heard a squeal of brakes and the sound of metal on metal but was too busy wielding a large branch to witness the Merc crash into the unmarked police car, which had been following the lorry.

She was already photographing the prostrate Paco by the time Gonzales rushed over to her.

'Are you hurt?'

'Of course not, but he might have a bit of a headache. Must have caught his head on something. Good job you made me stay in the trees!'

He smiled and shook his head.

'What can I say? Steve told me you were wasted as a journalist!'

A Brush with Chemistry

Tony Carter

As with so many interests I've had in my life, it was my parents who introduced me to chemistry. I think it was Christmas 1948 and my main present was a chemistry set. This was years before health and safety, of course, and I was thrilled and spent the day reading the accompanying book.

Then came the experiments. Wonderful fun. From my friends, I found out that a great variety of chemicals could be bought from the local *Boots The Chemist*. The liquids were supplied in small bottles and sometimes they had to be measured out. The powders and crystals were scooped out of larger containers and poured into small paper bags just as sweets would be.

After stink-bombing the local Woolworths with a dye that was totally indelible and burning a hole in the curtains, the chemistry set was confined to the loft. (In 1948 nothing was thrown away).

Fast forward to 1950 and, at the age of twelve, I was elevated to a senior house at my boarding school. Chemistry remained a favourite hobby and I kept my potions in a locker in the common room.

Then came the day when I decided to make a bomb, not with any evil intent, but purely as an experiment. First the container had to be procured. That came in the form of an empty *Vim* container.

The ingredients were essentially those of high-compact gunpowder. Added to this were the contents of a few .303 cartridges from our army cadet range. The detonator was a firework banger inserted down through the lid. As I have said, I had no evil intent. I simply wanted to see what the effect would be of this mix and quantity of chemicals.

Whilst I pondered this, I kept the device in my *wooden* locker sometimes, during power cuts it would have a candle on top!

Eventually the senior boys in the house got to hear about *Carter's bomb* and one day they demanded that I hand it over to them. *Oh no!* It wasn't meant to be like this, but I had no option and, when I duly took it out of my locker, they grabbed it and disappeared quickly.

There was nothing I could do, but I didn't have to wait long…

Suddenly, there was an almighty bang and the windows shook and the doors rattled. Within a few minutes the housemaster, a burly Yorkshireman named Hodgson, bellowed out my name and I went into his study. After a dressing-down, I received a very painful six strokes of the cane on my rear end but, as I left his office, his tone changed and he asked about my mixture of chemicals.

I later discovered the senior boys had placed the device behind our house, in the hole, on the eighteenth green on the school golf course. It had blown a three-foot crater, in depth and diameter, and as a consequence I was subject to the wrath of the school groundsman!

For some time after I was known as *Carter the bomb*!

Five years later, I was saying my farewells and my mother and father had bought a present for Mr Hodgson. I knocked on his study door and as I said goodbye, I passed him a parcel.

He smiled. 'I do hope it doesn't explode!'

*

What a different story would be written today, so as a short tongue-in-cheek postscript...

There was an explosion. The housemaster phoned the police who, despite being undermanned, sent ten cars, including firearms and anti-terrorist units. Emilia Fox of Silent Witness was first on the scene. Bomb disposal, ambulance and fire brigade were also in attendance. Carter was in custody. All lockers and wardrobes were searched. Emilia Fox and her team examined the crater and declared that it had, indeed, been a bomb. Housemaster Hodgson was put under protection but later he was sacked for allowing bombs to be made in his boarding house. The BBC carried the story for a week, blaming the Tory government for being so lenient with bombers (and schools).

Breaking News

Linda Burton-Cooper

Breaking news! Breaking news!
Hurricane Strength Winds
Causing havoc in Mexico!
Warning: Acapulco Flooded!

The radio warning spurred Esteban Rodriguez on even faster to secure his precious retails stock out of way of the water seeping in under the shop front entrance and out of the sight of those grasping Looters.

A loud commotion from the street drowned the broadcaster's voice. People were frantically running either side of the kerb and shouting in panic. 'What is it now?' he tutted, studiously trying to ignore the kerfuffle outside.

His breathless plump form scampered hurriedly up and down the stepladder putting the most expensive designer handbags on the top display shelf, out of immediate view and the invading water.

Esteban Rodriguez was the owner of the foremost designer handbag shop in the most salubrious shopping area in the whole of Acapulco and to validate his status above his shop in gold calligraphy was written…

Rodriguez Designer Handbags est.1968,
The No.1 Supplier of Designer handbags
In the whole of Acapulco.

The noisy frantic crowd were now shouting, squealing and hopping around more or less outside his shop front entrance.

'*¿madre mia, que pasa fuera?*' What's going on out there?'

Looking through the door he could see the crowd now filled with fear and awe huddled together on either side of the pavements.

Unable to see above them he stepped onto his ladder, peering over their heads. There in full view, to his sublime amazement, he saw her!

She was wading down the centre of the road, her tail flailing and lashing out from side to side, her mouth agape, the dappled sunlight highlighted the iridescence of her scaled green, blue flank.

Esteban's nose twitched with excitement and rubbing his hands together, he tried to estimate how long she was. 'She must be over 3 metres,' he gasped, at which point his imagination began to run riot. He could see crocodile skin handbags, wallets, sunglass cases and even cute little lipstick holders. Her teeth and claws would make toggles. And, and… he wallowed with delight.

He was breathless. Even the adored Mexican top model, the exotic Dolores Cachua wearing nothing but designer handbags could not look more beautiful in his eyes than she did; this enormous crocodile.

But how could he capture this wonderful assortment of accessories? He'd seen the *Crocodile Dundee* movies but he, Esteban Rodriguez, was a small and homely man and the tools of his trade were needle and thread.

Everyone started and turned to the loud rumbling sound coming from father down the street. Trundling toward them at a watery pace they saw the purpose built motorised barrow of some 3 metres long headed by a team of men carrying thick sturdy rope. Within seconds the team of able men had lassoed the flailing creature, bound its gaping mouth and angry tail and with great effort and at great risk to themselves, they loaded her onto the barrow and set off to transport her back to her normal habitat, the river.

Esteban's sad eyes met with the trussed up crocodile's glinting half-mast gaze and she seemed to speak to him.

'Sorry, Esteban. I know you could have made great things of me.'

Breaking new! Breaking news!
Crocodile seen cruising down the main shopping street in Acacpulco!!

A Bédar Summer

Tony Carter

The aromas drift upon a light breeze
Wafting through the rustling trees,
With jasmine, orange blossom and herbs,
Very quietly…the peace is not disturbed.
This tranquil place on the mountainside
Over which the lower clouds glide.
Bédar's origins from so long ago,
A village before the Moors
Were forced to go.
The mines were worked by many men
Toiling so far underground, way back then.
Times were hard, the rewards were small,
Food was meagre or not at all.
But the village survived the difficult times
And the later wars in these warm climes.
Finally things improved
And the village became home
To many who had been forced to roam.
Then a donkey brays, a distinctive he-haw,
An oriole's fluted trills, the grunting boar,
The church clock chimes morning hour,
Sounds which shudder the ancient tower.
For peace, contentment Bédar's the place
That takes one's life to a slower pace.

Printed in Great Britain
by Amazon